...AND WHERE THE WIND SPUN THEM

...AND WHERE THE WIND SPUN THEM

BOOK ONE: CENTRIFUGAL FORCE

G.E.M. MUNRO

TAN*GENT*BOOKS, INC.

IGRAN

SIMAN

ISBN: 978-0-9688886-3-6

Tangent Books, Inc.,

Box 51,

Hagensborg, BC

V0T1H0

Tangent Books is a publishing concern of Amarok Society.

AmarokSociety.org/Subscribe

Cover and interior illustrations by G.E.M. Munro.

Preface

I push my way once again through the forbidding borders of this overgrown garden, through the bony clutching fingers of its outer branches, through the jagged tripwires of its undergrowth; I lift my feet high, I press ahead elbows-first, but there's no escaping the wounds of its bramble and briar thorns.

I didn't plant this mess; I suppose someone or some force did, and then wove it into this ugly deathweb; this is the found-swatch theory: anything material this disordered and careless proves that devils do indeed exist. I didn't plant this mess, but I've for some time been haunted by whatever may be my duty to tidy it, so I push my way into it once again.

And, amazing, gleaming there at my torn knee, between the stalks and thistles and withered befouled leaves and shrivelled aborted buds, in the little extended fingers of a small sapling, reaching out through the terrible tangle, is a pure and clean blue berry, like a miracle marble or a perfect little world; and just there at my thigh is a red pepper, and over there a dark hard nut, and there, alas, a stunted, bitter jackfruit; and I pick them all without apology, for this fruit is grown to be plucked, to be carried elsewhere, to the wider world.

The wider world is you: I put this fruit in a crude clay bowl, to depict it in an arrangement I hope may appeal to your sensibility; but carrying it from where it grew, or arranging it within a bowl, doesn't make it less real. It's still life, still what was growing, still what I've found.

Book One

Centrifugal Force

Do you know where two seeds may spurt
Of fruit dashed down by mad monkey thrilled,
So to sprout bare upon that self-same dirt
Where parents' blood and bile was spilled?
One absorbs it all to poisoned hurt
While one absorbs it all to be fulfilled.
      - verse purportedly written by div-dir hands.

A little boy rich in imagination and utterly poor in everything else finds a portion of a plastic ball, like some emptied reptile egg, discarded at the roadside and tries to kick it along as he tags behind his older sister.

The road is filthy with dust and dried effluent of overflowed open sewers and other accumulations to defy delicate analysis, and the grime on the torn scrap of ball mutes the colours of its manufacture. It doesn't present a bright prospect, but, still, the boy hopes for a moment's fun as he kicks it with his dirty little bare foot. His imagination kicks, too, as the flapping empty ball seems too closely to echo aspects of his hunger. However, he shoots it forward to the feet of his sister. She regards it with brief disdain.

The boy is named Siman, and he is seven years old; he has spent most of that time in a state of hunger, a state of awareness, desperation and an old resignation acquired when his baby wails obtained nothing, or nothing enough. Like his sister, Igran, who is nine years old, he is wearing everything he owns: a pair of shorts and a torn t-shirt, the faded legend of which he has no hope of ever being able to read; Igran is wearing a tattered dress that's too big for her, and a long shawl of thin, limp cotton she stole from a jute clothesline.

The stolen shawl isn't any robin hood affair: that reputation lies years in their future; at present, Igran doesn't rob the rich to give to the poor; she robs the poor to give to the poorer, herself and her brother. She knows from emphatic personal experience that the poor haven't any recourse through the law, not as the rich have, and it is much less fretful to pilfer from the poor.

She steps over the ball and appears to be giving it no further notice, but, at the last possible moment, she strikes backward with her heel, sends it flying flopping into the piled litter that lines the road. Siman chases after it, and neatly pivots to send it forward to his sister again. This might be sport.

Of course, such a pivot is one of the obvious ones, so one of the unimportant ones: the critical pivots of one's life are harder to identify and recognize: in Siman's short life, the pivotal point, that moment when all his meagre possibilities were apparently destroyed, might have been any one of several on that terrible day of two years earlier. Was it Igran's deception? Their father's careless slip? Or was it an ongoing element of his life that suddenly fully manifested itself: was it their father's peaceful, genial nature? Their mother's acrimonious mentality? Or was it an event that would seem to have little to do with them, but the extrapolations of which made a beeline to intersect their lives? A case could be made for any. And was that other moment, that instance of wonder that followed, that infused a hopeless boy with unreasonable hope, the pivot of his life?

That his pivot to send the partial ball forward to Igran again is one of the trivial ones is indisputable, though. Igran sneers at it as it lands, inert, at her feet.

"I'm not going to play with that crummy thing," she says.

Siman says "It would be better if we could stuff something in it."

"Your head would be better if we could stuff something in it," she says. "And my belly."

He briefly scans the roadside's accumulated rubbish for a suitable stuffing material, as though it might yield something more than rat-rot babies, then pulls off his t-shirt, bundles it, and crams it into the shell of the ball. He drops the ball to his feet, gives it an experimental kick; it's about as lively and responsive as a bald, dead dog, but he dribbles it forward, anyway, runs circles around Igran several times.

"There's a stupid little fly buzzing around my head," she says. "I'll have to swat it."

"Try," Siman taunts.

He doesn't laugh at her failed efforts as he spins around her, but he allows himself a smile, and even this is too much of pride-goeth-before-a-foul, as Igran finally catches him with a kick to his shin, and he trips and sprawls before her.

"Oops," she says.

"Oof," he says, sitting up and rubbing his leg and elbows in turn. "No fair."

"You poke a sleeping cobra, it wakes up," Igran says. "What's no fair about that?"

He decides, anyway, that warmth is a more pressing priority than either football or its justice, and he retrieves his shirt, and pulls it on as he follows behind Igran.

Their land is tropical, but not equatorial, and the night just past had been cold for them, and, on the asphalt footpath where they'd lain huddled together, Igran had fussed through the night to keep them both covered by the light shawl, had cooed and sung to him through her own violent shivers.

In a little mahogany tree, birds he couldn't name sing down to him now. Others call them magpie robins, but they're neither magpies nor robins; they are an otherwise unnamed type of thrush, small, black and white, and sweet singers. Siman raises his face and sings back to them, and Igran snorts.

Early morning in this enormous city is the time for birds and little urchins, when the roads are bare and quiet, before the press and din of pedestrians and traffic cast aside children of no purpose and overwhelm birdsong, still when the day seems to promise something it subsequently fails to deliver.

"Let's check out Ortalt Avenue," he suggests.

"The street sweepers will have been there already."

"Maybe not yet," he says. "If we hurry…"

At night on busy Ortalt Avenue, several vendors wheel carts in front of the stalls and shops to peddle snacks like spicy puffed rice or stingy sunflower seeds or hard little fried kernels of this or that, set out in appealing display on sectioned trays, to be scooped into small paper packets for the impulsively peckish, and sometimes some spills to the footpath, and sometimes wealthy young women ask their escorts to purchase a packet, pick at it with enamelled and ringed fingers just enough to satisfy their tiny craving, then drop it, unconcerned; and if Igran and Siman get to Ortalt early enough, sometimes the morning's birds or street sweepers don't find the spilled stuff before the children do.

So they hurry, to the extent that they ever really hurry when they aren't making their getaway, until they happen to come to a certain building of flats, named something grand, Royal Towers, and as they come to it, Igran sighs in impatient recognition, and Siman stops, as he'd always stopped when he came to that building, and he turns his eyes up to its roof, searches silently, but keenly, for what he'd seen there, before, during those nightmare days of two years earlier.

He puts his hand to his brow in grief and wonder.

"You're as crazy as she is," Igran hisses angrily.

"I know what I saw," he says.

That, however, isn't the strict truth; knowing that he'd seen something doesn't mean that he knows what he saw.

"I thought we were going to hurry."

He is incapable of hurrying, however, and she curses herself for overlooking where they were approaching, and she drops herself onto her haunches, squats and fumes. He stands gazing upward.

"Just as crazy as she is…"

But, in his imagination, Siman has become chronologically unpinned again, braces himself for the terrible trip backward, as if he's been kicked back by fate's heel just as it seemed about to step beyond him.

He lands with a flaccid plop on the dirt pathway of the huge, impossibly crowded slum of his birth.

And there stood Igran, seven years old, dressed, as Siman was, in any t-shirt and any cotton shorts, amid other children and a pair of skinny, skinny dogs of dreadful bald patches, stood on the narrow path between the tiny hovels, the wall of one the wall of the next, and she leaned with sincerity toward Fannel, a boy of her age.

"It's who can throw a stone the farthest," Igran said.

Fannel cocked his head with sour humour. "You against me?"

"Right, me against you."

"You think I can't beat a girl?"

"Maybe some other girl," she said.

Fannel glanced about himself, to the other children gathered around them, and laughed.

"What do I win?" he asked.

Igran called out to five year old Siman, who watched from a short distance with some dismay.

"Siman, come here."

He pushed through the little ring to join his sister.

"Show Fannel those marbles."

Instinctively, he shoved his hand into the pocket of his shorts.

"No," he said firmly. "Daddy gave me ---."

"I'm not going to lose them," she said. "You know that no one in the world can throw a stone as far as me."

The other children laughed aloud.

"Just show Fannel the marbles," she said.

With reluctance, Siman pulled his little hand from his pocket, and cradled within it were several marbles his father had bestowed upon him with delight some days before. His father had had quite a good day on Ortalt Avenue, where he set up an old chair at the roadside and tied a dangerous piece of broken mirror to a lamp pole and offered cheap haircuts and shaves, and on his way home he'd seen a small plastic bag of marbles at a stall by the edge of the slum, and had splurged. For Siman to have a bag of marbles was akin to having the only walkie-talkie in town: he didn't know of any other boys with such a treasure as marbles, so he had no one to play with or against, but that was of no matter to him. To Siman, they were jewels to be enjoyed for their beauty and the marvel of their formation, and he had no intention of ever risking them in a game.

"Only those?" Fannel said.

"How many do you have now?" Igran said.

"All right, what do you win?"

"Oh, I don't know," she said offhandedly. "Your top, I guess."

For days, she had stood over crouched boys, watching them playing with Fannel's plain little wooden top, and her natural exclusion from boys' games had begun to eat at her insides, so that she eventually panted with fury at every toss of the top, as the boys seemed to move their shoulders to obscure from her even the sight of its spin.

But she was all carefree and casual as she posited the wager.

"No," said Fannel. "Not my top for those crummy marbles."

Siman couldn't quite understand the crudity of someone who could value a dirty top over the round gems he held, and he regarded both Fannel and his sister with woe.

"Okay," she said lightly. "So, you're admitting to everyone you can't throw a stone as far as a girl."

And she started away, taking Siman's arm.

"Where are you going?" Fannel said. "Did I say I wouldn't take your stupid marbles?"

So, the competition was arranged. It was established by Siman's refusal to give up his marbles that he would hold both prizes, and Fannel tossed him the top. Siman was confused as to what was required of him. The other children rooted about until each competitor held in hand not stones, really, but roughly comparable bits of broken brick.

"No, no," Igran sternly instructed the children still clustered around them, "you all need to stand down the sides of the foot path, to see how far the stones go. Mine, I know, will go very far, so you need to go far along."

So authorized, the children went along, and Siman started to go with them.

"No, Siman, you stand behind us because you hold the bets," Igran said, and Fannel nodded as though he were experienced in such matters.

Fannel threw first, as that was the privilege of his sex, and he grunted as he threw.

The stone travelled far enough to make Siman grip his marbles more tightly.

The children down the path cheered.

"That, uh," Fannel said, almost apologetically, "I could have thrown that better..."

Igran took a stance, one thin little leg forward, her thin little throwing arm set back behind her, and she pointed high above the horizon with her free left hand.

The suspense was more than Fannel could bear, apparently, and he cried sharply, "Hey, Igran, can you throw farther than mine?!", just as Igran seemed at the instant of her release.

Igran shifted slightly, then repositioned herself, and once again, Fannel called just as she seemed ready to throw.

"Hey, are you going to throw now, Igran?!"

Again, Igran shifted.

"You can yell all you want, Fannel. It won't make any difference. I'll throw way farther than you, no trouble at all."

She took her stance, and then said, unmoving, "Watch the sky."

Suddenly she sprang, her right arm whipping forward, and all eyes were turned up to the direction to which her left hand still pointed.

Only Siman saw that she'd dropped her stone behind her before whipping her arm forward.

"Whoa!" she cried, pointing then with her right hand as children scanned the sky. "Did you see that?! It was fast, but you should have been able to see it, if you're sharp-eyed!"

"I saw it! I saw it!" cried one little boy. "It was in the sky!"

"I didn't see anything!" Fannel protested.

"You can still see it!" Igran said. "Look there!"

Fannel shielded his eyes with his hands, peering.

"There, at the horizon!" Igran cried.

"I see it!" another girl called.

The children searched the sky, and, as they did, Igran quickly reached down and grabbed her bit of brick in her left hand, swiftly and sharply struck Siman in the back of the head with it, and let it drop behind him.

Siman tried to be brave in his pain and surprise, but when Igran put her face before his and asked urgently, "What is it, Siman, what's the matter?", his resolved melted, and he let out a yelp.

Children were returning to the competitors, and they looked with interest, if not pity, to the injured boy.

"O, look!" said Igran, collecting a smudge of blood on her fingertip from Siman's head.

Then a little girl espied the brick piece, and drew attention to it.

"Wow!" cried Igran with delight, "I must have thrown it clear around the world, and it hit Siman when it got back!"

Some eyes widened, but Siman snuffled and Fannel scoffed.

"Clear around the world! Garbage!"

Igran fixed him with a sharp look, and addressed the other children: "Fannel doesn't even know the world is round. I suppose you think it's flat, Fannel."

Fannel gave off the atmosphere of a boy who'd never considered the shape of the world.

"I don't think...," he began.

"If the world isn't round, Fannel, then how could my stone go clear around it and hit Siman in the head? How could it go around a flat world?"

Some children who'd never considered the shape of the world nodded after a moment's thought.

"It could bend, sort of...," Fannel suggested.

"Fannel, the world is round. My father's newspaper showed a picture of it."

"Your father can't read!" Fannel countered. "My father can read!"

Fannel's father was one of the small handful of the slum's thousands of dwellers who could read, but not his own native language, only Dilli, the scriptural language of the Fannu religion. Igran's father occasionally brought home, as fire-starters, newspapers left at his chair by customers, and one paper, indeed, had carried a photograph of the world taken by satellite, and Siman had stretched the paper over the tiny space of their hovel's floor, and had placed his marbles around the world and stared at them all with rapture. He'd told Igran about the beautiful round world, and she'd seemed uninterested at the time.

"At least my father knows the world is round," Igran sneered. "At least he knows anything you send out this way will come around to you that way. He'd know that's how my stone hit Siman. What do you or your father know?" She grabbed the top from Siman, and held it over her head. "Who wants to play with me and my top?"

"Wait!" Fannel protested.

"Sorry, Fannel, you're not allowed," Igran said.

"Play with a girl?" asked another boy.

"If you want to play with a top, you'll play with a girl," she said.

"I'll play," offered a little girl.

Igran flickered with brief annoyance.

"Boys first," she said sternly.

She ran down the path, holding her prize high as she went, and the children chased after her as a victory throng.

Siman and Fannel were left there, with Siman carefully touching his head wound and staring at Fannel with some perplexity.

Fannel glumly watched the running children, then felt Siman's eyes on him.

"What are you looking at, idiot?" he demanded, and then he went and threw himself into a slouch against a sagging woven rush wall, wiping at his eyes roughly.

Troubled Siman went into the rabbit-warren side paths of the slum, along uneven bamboo walkways elevated over the boggy areas that constituted much of this illegal squatters' settlement. He was hoping to find his friend, Benamy.

Benamy was a girl of his own age, and she'd been born without eyes. Fannel's father would tell anyone, including Benamy, that her condition was a judgment on her father's weak and wicked ways. No one else had a better explanation, although Benamy had told Siman that she liked her father, and that he didn't seem so weak and wicked to her. Siman liked Benamy because she was sweet, herself, but also because she enjoyed talking about things, just as Siman did. He had known her odd appearance all his life, and thought nothing of it, although he did regret her absence of vision, because he found much of the world beautiful to see.

Benamy often sat in the doorway of her family's hovel and that was where Siman found her. He sat down beside her without greeting, and, as always, maybe from sound, maybe from smell, or maybe because no other child sat with her, she knew who he was.

"Some places, rich people have big festivals on their birthdays," she said. "Even some of the rich people in our homeland." Short lengths of straw were stuck into the little slits of what should have been her eyelids. Her parents did that on some advice from somewhere, possibly somewhere medical.

"What are birthdays?" he asked.

"Well, I don't know," she said. "I think it's the day rich babies come to their rich Mummy's."

"I don't think babies would like a festival on the day they come. It would be too noisy and scary; babies don't like loud things, even rich babies, probably."

"Maybe rich babies' ears don't work for a while."

"Baby cats' and dogs' eyes don't work for a while," Siman offered, nodding pointlessly.

"Maybe I'm a baby cat," she said.

"Maybe. Do you like to eat raw rats?"

"I don't know. I should try one. Could you get one for me?"

"No, Benamy, I was joking. I don't like even to see rats. It would be terrible to see you eat one."

"Maybe I should start with a raw mouse first, then, see how that goes," she said.

"Benamy, I was joking."

"So was I, Siman," she said. "I guess I'm not a baby cat. Do I look like one?"

"Not really." Siman reached up and rubbed his fingers behind her ear. "Do you like that?"

"Yes," she said.

"Well, then, who knows? Do you have a tail?"

"That would be good, to have a tail, wouldn't it?"

"Not if it were like a cat's tail or a dog's tail. All they do is give Fannel something to swing them by. A monkey tail, though..."

"Yes, I'd like to be a monkey," she said.

"Do you like to jump on people and bite them? Do you like to throw fruit down on people from trees?"

"I think maybe I don't," she said.

"Then you wouldn't like being a monkey. Anyway, I don't think I could ever be friends with a monkey."

"And I just remembered, monkeys eat something even worse than rats."

"What food could be worse than rats?" Siman asked.

She leaned over to him and whispered something close to his ear.

"No, eewwww," he cried, truly shocked. "They couldn't."

"So, I wouldn't ever want to be a monkey," she said.

Siman tried to turn his mind away, but his natural curiosity captured him. After some thought, he said, "I wonder if a monkey could start out with one meal, and then just keep eating it over and over again for the rest of its life."

"We eat the same meal over and over again," she said. "Rice and lentils, rice and lentils, rice and lentils..."

"I know we do, Benamy, but it's different rice and lentils, not the same ones."

"O, yes," she said, laughing.

He considered the possibility of what would amount to a perpetual motion macaque machine a while longer, thought that, if it were so, it made the monkeys' predilection for dashing perfectly good fruit down on passersunder, and their group raids to steal rice bowls from hungry children, even more culpable.

"Miners drink their pee," Benamy confided in a whisper.

"What are miners?" Siman whispered back.

"I don't know, but they drink their pee."

Siman had seen little flocks of mynas walking, stately and stiff-legged, along the lakeside, and had always found them to be very pretty birds, didn't sense in them anything suggesting future natural competitors for spilled grain, and he hoped it wasn't they that were offending against their dignity by drinking what shouldn't be drunk.

Unlike some boys his age, he wasn't keen on the subject of effluence, so he turned to affluence, instead.

"I think rich babies' ears probably work right away. They're rich, after all. They probably work better."

"Maybe it's a quiet festival on their birthdays," Benamy said. "I wonder what that would be like."

"You wouldn't even notice it, I guess."

"I'd notice it if there were more things to things to eat than rice and lentils," she said, still thinking about their own unvaried diet. "Eating fruit doesn't need to be noisy."

"It's noisy when monkeys eat it," he said. "Rich people have good things to eat every day, haven't they?"

"Maybe for quiet festivals, they just have more."

They both quietly chewed on that for a moment or two.

"Igran made a bet with my marbles," Siman said.

"Too bad," she sighed, genuinely unhappy. In recent days, Siman would put marbles in her hand and try to describe them as she rolled them.

"And then she lied to win the bet."

"So, you've still got the marbles?"

"Yes," he said. "But it's...."

"Who'd she bet against?"

"Fannel. She took his top."

Benamy raised her face to emphasize her happy smile.

"But it's not right, Benamy," he said. "I didn't say anything."

"So what? They're your marbles, not Igran's or Fannel's. You didn't bet them."

"But I let Fannel think he lost, and I knew he didn't. Daddy says I'll never have anything but honour, just like him. Honour is all I'll ever have."

"And marbles. Honour and marbles, Siman."

Benamy may have been saying what Siman would want to hear, but he fretted still, and thought he'd like to talk the matter over with his father, but for the trouble he'd create for himself with Igran. So, he tried to picture his father in the same sort of situation, but couldn't: his father led without any memorable opportunities to do so by example. Opportunities for anything good seemed very rare in the slum.

Benamy's parents returned from their daily bath in the small lake beside which the slum had sprung up like a poisonous mushroom. The lake had been made by high-minded planners, in a past age of much greater optimism, as a beauty feature of the city, before the city grew like cancer and poisoned itself and buried beauty beneath filth and false urgencies; the lake was impossibly polluted, in large part from the noxious flows from the slum, and the thousands of people who bathed in it less cleaned themselves than ensured that the slum's germs and toxins were equally distributed to all, an exercise of unusual liberality for that land. Some people chose to wash themselves by way of the water of the slum's single hand pump, but its well was significantly influenced by both the lake and the too-nearby single latrine, and it was of doubtful benefit, too. Some people actually referred to the place as 'Lakeview Slum', a name that wasn't wrong, but was too suggestive of the picturesque, thereby demonstrating the difference between accuracy and truth.

As her mother rung sewage from her hair and her father shook sewage from his ear, Benamy told them of Siman's little worry. Her mother responded that cheating was wrong, which contributed nothing, and then her father opined that Fannel's father, Malfren, along with his crackpot followers, already exacted enough from the people of the slum, with their intimidating demands for alms and tithes, and no one should yield anything to that family at any time.

That also failed to answer Siman and his slipped grip on his honour, his grasp of which as a concept was already fumbling enough, so he wandered away through the pathways between the cramped ramshackle hovels, weaving around loose toddlers and fuming clay ovens burning anything that could burn, and suspect puddles, weaving through tangled gossip and baby cries and music from a raspy radio, until finally he came upon Fannel sitting dejectedly where he would obstruct, and command pity, the most.

With deepest regret, Siman reached into his pocket and drew out his marbles.

He held them before Fannel's face. The older boy looked in brief confusion, then sprang up in fury, grabbed the marbles, and threw them scattering over and into the lake.

Siman watched the little rings from each marble spread over the green surface.

"And that's just the start!" Fannel hissed before stalking off.

Siman noticed anew how his head ached from Igran's stone strike, and his eyes started stinging, so he sank into a squat and rubbed his eyes, and tried to see, in his mind's stinging eye, something that wasn't beautiful marbles' arches into a fetid lake; he was unsuccessful.

So, he plumbed the miseries of honour without marbles, the experience of which exploration was quite like being a marble thrown into that lake.

In another few minutes, he was unable to prevent his imagination from picturing the pleasure of his father as he set into good-natured haggling with the stall owner over the price of the bag of marbles, his father surely sporting the same smile with which he later presented the marbles to his stunned son.

"Look," Daddy had said to Mummy at that time, "his eyes have grown to twice the size of the marbles!"

His father was a very good barber, but a poor businessman, Mummy often complained, because he would take so much time with each customer, gossiping and joking, snipping air or towelling chins long after the job was really done. "There's more to life than money," he would say. "There's more to life with money," Mummy would say.

Siman felt a great need to go home and climb onto his father's lap and hug him hard, seek and give comfort over the critically undisclosed loss of the marbles. So, he made his way through the passages toward his hovel, and as he neared it, a sickening sound came to him over the many other noises of many other lives in too-close proximity: it was the sound of his mother in one of her vitriolic rants. When he rounded a corner to the small square before his family's shanty, he saw that the quarrel was with Rachan, a young woman neighbour who'd always been friendly enough with Siman and Igran. One never knew what would set Mummy off, but she'd had a running resentment of Rachan for as long as Siman could remember; some in the slum surmised that Rachan's antagonism wasn't that she did anything wrong, but that she did something wonderfully right: she was absolute mistress of extraordinarily expressive, sensuous dance of her own invention; she could transfix men, women, children all for an hour or more, to the scratchy strains from any old radio; Mummy, more beautiful than anyone, might have seen Rachan as her chief feminine rival for admiration in the slum; Mummy was laying in with rapid-fire denunciation of some immediate grievance Siman could typically not construe; he spent no time trying to understand her, as he'd found the attempt to be utterly useless in the past. Rachan was giving almost as good as she got, though, which was remarkable, because most people considered battles with Mummy were lost from the outset, and would walk away with a dismissive wave. Some other neighbours were gathered to watch, and Siman spotted Fannel among them, and Daddy was there, too, remonstrating and smiling and trying to insert placating words between the verbal volleys. At one point, he took hold of Mummy's arm and began to guide her to the doorway of their hovel, but Mummy, inspired by some renewed fury, then jerked her arm away and spun to stalk back to Rachan, her hips in exaggerated sway, to shake her finger before Rachan's nose and shake her hands over her head and to shake her head back and forth so that her lustrous dark hair flew out behind her, all the while spitting out a diatribe of condemnation. Rachan just smiled furiously back at her for some time, thrusting out her hip and setting her hand on it.

Where others observed with silent interest or concern, Fannel seemed most entertained by it, grinned and laughed aloud.

Daddy finally stopped smiling, himself, and made to grab his wife's arm again, but just as he did, Mummy shot her arm down, and Rachan shot her arm up to gesture in conviction of Mummy's insanity, and Daddy accidently grabbed Rachan's arm instead of Mummy's.

There were sharp expressions of concern from the watching neighbours. Rachan, Mummy and Daddy each looked down to Daddy's frozen hand in shock. Fannel's laughter screeched like a giddy monkey's.

There was no question that a man touching any woman other than his wife was a transgression against the dictates of the Fannu religion; how serious a transgression it was was a matter of interpretation, and, to an extent, a matter of in which stream of Fannu the interpreter stood.

Fannu is a polytheistic religion, with a number of gods credited with specific instances of creation and responsible for specific elements of existence. It wasn't endemic to this land, but had arrived several hundred years earlier, carried from far away on horseback and delivered at sword point. While its success in the land had been based on expedience and survival impulse and the relative lassitude of the native belief system it supplanted, belief in Fannu was soon sincere enough; even sincere belief had options of emphasis, though, because of the array of deities available, any of which might, conventionally, be stressed with equal virtue.

Two of Fannu's gods received the greatest reverence and ostensible obedience, and were generally acknowledged to be the leading lights in the Fannu firmament: Pakron, which has the form of a goat and is the god primarily concerned with human matters, and is often depicted as being tolerant of humanity and somewhat forgiving of its multiplicity of errors; and Pazich, which has the form of a monkey, is concerned with the systems, including justice and fate, of Earth and the Universe. In Its dealings with humanity It is strict and critical of humanity's failure to function obediently within Its systems.

It might be observed that the choice of which of the two gods to affix one's main adherence was less a matter of belief than which of the gods more closely matched one's own nature. So, Daddy, for instance, adhered to the more patient Pakron, while Fannel's father, Malfren, was a fervent advocate of Pazich, and, it so happened, a local leader of a new element, sect, really, of the religion. In a distant land, a new holy man had arisen who claimed to have been visited by a messenger of Pazich bearing a warning to wayward humanity: Pazich, fed up with humanity's iniquity and its interference with the smooth operation of Pazich's systems, had concluded that humanity had strayed because of Pakron's negligent disinclination to deal with sin strictly and harshly enough to be instructional; so, to preserve the all-important systems, and coincidentally preserve humanity, Pazich the monkey had slit the throat of Pakron the goat, and then had devoured Pakron's corpse whole. The holy man favoured with this information was named Heldin, and Heldin had ever since relayed the news with frequent extrapolations and judgments of what it meant and by what conventions the new ethereal order should be observed and worshipped.

And Malfren was as zealous and evangelical a Heldinite as anyone, anywhere. Like any strict Heldinite, he never shaved the beard of his chin, but braided it to represent the goat tail of Pakron protruding from Pazich's sacred monkey mouth, the last of the vanquished god to be seen as it was so properly swallowed, and he always carried on his hip the ceremonial dagger commemorative of that with which Pazich so justifiably slit Pakron's throat. Malfren had vigorously recruited (browbeaten, Benamy's father would say) new adherents, and had come to bestride the slum of his humble origins in righteous arbitration and suitable hauteur.

Heldin demanded of each head of a Heldinite family the ritual slaughter, with the ceremonial dagger, of a goat on the many holy days: this was an onerous responsibility to the extremely poor of this land, along with the demanded tithes, and many Heldinites had fallen into deep debt to goat merchants, of which Malfren had quickly become the most prosperous, locally. Heldin, it was said, was of the practice of swallowing his sacrificial goat whole, as Pazich had done, and two of the slum's faithful had actually died attempting to follow his example, and their martyrdom was celebrated. (Benamy's father would say they'd chosen death over another of Malfren's endless sermons and diatribes broadcast across the slum by loudspeakers.)

So, when Daddy accidently grabbed Rachan's arm, the reaction of those watching to the indisputably improper action was governed by their personal fealty to which god.

"A thousand times, I beg your pardon," Daddy gasped when able to speak. "I had no intention...."

Rachan, herself, obviously hadn't embraced the strict new doctrine, for she laughed the matter off, saying to Mummy, "See, even your own husband would prefer to take me home."

This further enflamed Mummy, but Daddy made no mistake, grabbing her by both arms and firmly pulling her to their shanty.

Mummy's continuing invective could be easily heard from within, but people treated the episode as concluded and returned to their own mundane occupations: but they were wrong, for, as Siman observed, young Fannel departed with red-faced urgency along the passage to his own father's hovel.

Siman ventured into his mean home when the volume from within it diminished. Mummy lay on her side on the one hard bed, sobbing and muttering as Daddy rubbed her back and shoulders and said soft comforting things.

"It's because I'm too beautiful," Mummy cried. "That's why they hate me."

"I know, dear," said Daddy. "Everyone knows you are beautiful."

Siman felt Mummy wasn't at her most beautiful just at that moment, but he certainly found her compellingly so when her face wasn't so florid and moist.

"But people don't hate you," Daddy continued. "Your beauty is a pleasure to them, I'm sure."

"Everyone's so cruel to me," Mummy sobbed. "Everyone's so unfair."

"I don't think they mean to be cruel," Daddy said. "Maybe they just make mistakes in their behaviour."

In time, Mummy, war weary, fell into a doze, and, even so, Daddy sat beside her, stroking her head and hair. Siman sat on the floor and felt the loss of his marbles.

Several figures appeared in silhouette in the doorway.

"Brother, we will speak to you!" commanded one, whom Siman recognized as Malfren.

"Please, brother," Daddy hushed, rising quickly and stepping to the doorway. "Let my poor wife sleep."

"We will speak to you of a matter of grave importance!"

"Certainly, brother, but quietly, outside."

Daddy stepped through the door, and was immediately seized by the arms by two of the dozen or so men accompanying Malfren.

Siman leapt up and followed as Malfren and his Heldinites conducted Daddy brusquely along, collecting a train of curious and concerned neighbours as they went, until they came to a relatively open space by the main pathway of the slum.

"Brother, what's the matter?" Daddy kept asking. "What is it?"

Malfren offered no explanation, but motioned the men holding Daddy to turn him to face those who were following and gathering around the space. The Heldinites formed a semicircle around them. Malfren paced stiff-legged as the other slumdwellers collected.

Siman stepped forward and, dry-mouthed and high-voiced, said "Let Daddy go!"

"No, son, don't be upset," Daddy said, smiling down. "We come here to talk, that's all."

But Malfren looked down his nose at the little boy, and gestured to another man to remove Siman. The man took hold of Siman's arm and Siman struggled and wriggled against his grasp.

"For shame!" cried Benamy's father, who stepped forward from the crowd. "Are you Heldinites planning to torture children, now?"

The man holding Siman withered a bit in the glare, and let his grip loosen enough for Siman to squirm free and run to hug Daddy's leg.

"Brothers! Brothers!" Malfren shouted suddenly, raising his hands high. "We are here to save you, not torture you! We are here to save you from your sin!"

"What sin?" Benamy's father demanded.

"Are you so corrupted that a brazen defilement of a worthy woman means nothing to you?" Malfren thundered.

"What defilement?" Daddy asked.

"This man, this wicked man, defiled an innocent woman in plain sight of you all, and you did nothing, such is your own iniquity! By what authority do you forgive such sin?"

"But, brother, if you are speaking of Rachan, that was an accident," Daddy said. "Everyone saw I meant nothing ---."

"By what authority do you condemn a simple accident?" Benamy's father asked.

"I am not the authority!" Malfren cried to all. "Fannu is the authority! Pazich is the authority! Who will dare to dispute that?! Who will dispute the laws against corruption of women?!"

"I am not corrupted, if you are speaking of me!" said Rachan from the crowd.

Malfren had many times railed against Rachan's displays of depraved dancing, and she seemed to be innocent at his convenience.

"So says the corrupted woman! So says the corrupted tongue of the corrupted woman!"

Malfren paced back and forth furiously.

"You all saw the foul misdeed! But you've gone so far astray, none of you did anything in defence of virtue. Only an innocent child, my own son, Fannel, his eye not yet sullied by your wicked weakness, saw the truth of the sin, and sought justice for it!"

Heldinites shook fists and shouted in support. "Bless the innocent child Fannel!" some called.

"Are the virtuous strong to tolerate the sin of the wicked weak? Will not Pazich also condemn those who tolerate sin? Didn't Pazich set the sacred example of our salvation through the sacrificial execution of Pakron?"

Great cries of both "No!" and "Yes!" came from Malfren's glaring supporters, perhaps confused as to which question they should answer in their fervour.

"But, brother---," Daddy protested, smiling still.

"Do you repent your depraved sin?!" Malfren cried, wheeling suddenly to Daddy, his goat-tail braided beard whipping from side to side.

"I will repent any depraved sin, sure, brother. But I don't ---."

"Then will you, by your sacrifice, rescue those you have adulterated by your wicked weakness?!"

"What do you mean, adulterated?" asked Benamy's father.

"What do you mean, sacrifice?" asked Daddy.

"If you will not save yourselves," Malfren shouted generally, "you make it necessary for me to save you!"

What motivated what happened next? Perhaps Malfren had a special hatred for a popular man who spent his days happily shaving off the beards that should have been righteously grown and braided and swishing like tails. Whatever the motivation, Malfren told the men holding Daddy to hold him tightly, which prompted Daddy finally to struggle against them, and then Malfren drew his ceremonial dagger, stepped behind Daddy, and then the barber, whose pride was that he never nicked any man's throat, had his throat slit from ear to ear.

Siman, still hugging Daddy's leg, didn't see what Malfren had done, but he was thrown to the ground when Daddy dropped to his knees. The now-ashen men who held Daddy lowered him the rest of the way to the dirt gently, as though they didn't want him to be hurt.

When Siman discovered what was happening, when he threw himself across Daddy's shoulders and tried with his little hands to hold all the blood in, Daddy raised his dimming eyes to his son and mouthed a word. That was just before sight went swimming in Siman's eyes, before all breath departed father and son together, so that neither could even scream.

Standing over them, Malfren raised his hands in a posture of triumph.

"Death to the wicked weak!"

If he'd expected rabid echoes from his rabble, he was surprised. This event was, apparently, enough to curdle even their hot blood, and the Heldinites stared dumbfounded as the shocked silence broke to women's sobs and mews and men's growing cries of outrage.

Malfren's elbows seemed to weaken as the non-Heldinite men advanced upon him, and his golden tongue darted over his lips, but he was then seized by inspiration, either holy or otherwise.

"I didn't do that!" he cried, eyes wide. "I did not move my hand! It was divinely directed!"

The enraged men hesitated.

"Is it anything but a miracle?!" Malfren cried. "Heaven has acted through my hand! My hand was divinely directed!"

Heldinites were stirred. Non-Heldinites faltered in confusion, not prepared to punish Heaven.

Suddenly, though, little Igran squirmed through the crowd. She stopped for a moment's assessment, saw the combined form of her father and brother, Malfren's bloody dagger held aloft; then, with a sort of shrieking growl issuing through her bared teeth, and, heedless of his dagger, she flew at and up Malfren's chest and clawed savagely at his face. Malfren responded with a noise very like Igran's, quite as shrill, until his nearest supporters came to themselves and grabbed Igran, tore her from him and threw her back to the crowd.

She landed on her back, the breath knocked out of her, and she looked up to see, grinning down on her, Fannel, Malfren's innocent child, whose eye at that moment seemed far from unsullied by wickedness.

Malfren was rushed away by clustered supporters, as though the blood of his cheek and brow was the real sanguine emergency.

Benamy's mother, weeping, gathered Igran up into her arms and carried her away, as Benamy's father, his hands trembling, gently but firmly pried Siman from Daddy's corpse.

"Brother," sobbed a man standing nearby, "don't take him to his mother covered in her husband's blood. Take him to your house to clean him first."

Benamy's father nodded, then choked out, "We can't leave this unanswered, brother."

"Yes," another man said softly, "but not today. We've seen enough blood for one day."

Siman studied the ground from over the shoulder of Benamy's father as he was carried, noted how sharply everything was delineated in his vision's return, how distinct was the form and the shadow of the bit of brick Igran had dropped to the clay, how the dog paw print in the damp clay by the sparkling crystal puddle might have been a moon crater for its crisp relief, and noted how important every detail, how critical every rusted pock of a corrugated tin wall, seemed as he bumped along, how unbearably beautiful everything seemed and how breath no longer seemed necessary to sustain him, as though pain were an adequate substitute for air.

Benamy sat on her doorstep as her father stepped carefully by her into the house, and Siman thought he had so much, such sharp vision, Benamy might well have half of it, and he'd be relieved by its loss.

"Siman," said Benamy, apparently still considering wealth's plenty, "did you know that in some places they just squeeze the juice out of fruit and then throw the fruit away? All they want is just the juice. Did you know that?"

"No," Siman said. He wondered how much just juice fruit might contain, if its amount would be stunningly copious, and if, once it began to flow, it would be impossible to stop.

Her father set Siman down by the plank counter/table at the side wall of the shanty, and poured water from a plastic bottle into an aluminum basin.

"Here, son, put your hands in here."

Siman did that and watched Daddy's blood curl away into the clear water like the swirls on a marble. The man gently, carefully scooped water over Siman's quivering arms, and soon the bowl seemed all blood.

"Berkel's coming," Benamy said, and in a moment a man stood in the doorway.

"Brother," Berkel said, "the Heldinites are stringing the body up beside the footpath. They're hoisting him upside down, by his ankles. They say he's to serve as an example to all the wicked weak."

Benamy's father said nothing, but sat on the bed, and drew Siman onto his lap, and wept into Siman's hair.

"What is this world we've brought you into?" he gasped at last.

Berkel shifted on his feet, and said, "Brother, what should we do?"

Benamy's father had no reply, shook his head, and Berkel shuffled away.

In time, he delivered Siman to the boy's own hovel; a hundred people or more were collected about it; Igran was sitting on the floor inside, hugging her knees and watching Benamy's mother, who sat on the edge of the bed, holding Mummy's hand; Mummy lay on her side, her eyes closed.

Siman fell into a squat beside Igran.

Benamy's mother rose and went to her husband just outside the door, and they exchanged whispers.

Siman heard Benamy's father say, "We can't. She's unfit. She'll never be fit. You know."

And Benamy's mother said, "But we haven't enough for ourselves, already, Pakron knows.", and Benamy's father, stung, lowered his head and turned away, and then left. His wife watched him go, and, with a starting backward turn to the hovel, then spun and chased after him.

Siman and Igran sat and watched Mummy lying there for the longest time.

"Should one of us hold her hand?" Siman asked eventually.

"What for?" Igran said after a pause. "She's the one who's asleep."

"Maybe it would help her, anyway."

"What's going to help us?" Igran asked. "Not her, that's for sure."

Siman took his sister's hand in his. Bits of Malfren's face were still beneath her fingernails.

"Daddy said something to me, then," Siman said, after quelling his heaving heart at the very thought of saying so. "It was the last thing."

"What did he say?"

"I don't know. It was just one word. It started with mmm."

"Mummy?"

"No," he said. "It wasn't Mummy, I don't think."

"Murder," Igran said.

"Maybe."

They sat in silent consideration.

"I think it was more like marvel," Siman offered eventually.

"Marvel? Why would he say that?"

"I don't know," Siman said.

They sat like that a long time, hand in hand, until they, too, fell into a sleep, but Siman's was one he'd rather not have had. Time and again, Malfren was swinging through a tree like a monkey, dashing the tree's fruit to the ground, so that the juice of the fruit ran into crystal puddles, and the pulp was left to rot in enormous piles that glistened and turned black.

In the morning, they were awakened where they sat by Mummy clattering their few pots and bottles and plastic plates and cups onto the bed.

"Get up," she said to them. "We're going."

"What do you mean, going?" Igran asked.

"We can't stay here. Rachan has turned the whole slum against me."

"It isn't Rachan," Igran said. "It's Fannel and Malfren."

"Oh, it's Rachan. It's Rachan. Get going, and help me pack up. I'm too good for this place, anyway, and they hate me for that."

Siman felt Mummy, at that moment, didn't really look too good for anywhere. She was pale and perspiring, and her long hair was wet and plastered about her face, and her face seemed to have lost its muscles: her eyes were gaping, and her cheeks were hollow, and her mouth was always open, her lower lip grey, limp and sagging.

Siman had nothing of his own to add to the little pile of their belongings. Igran had only her ill-gotten top, which she pulled from the pocket of her shorts and threw onto the blanket. Siman stared at it, frozen, the top of the mourning to him, and Igran noticed.

"The top didn't start it. It's not my fault," she whispered angrily. "Don't you dare think it is!"

The question arose, however, of why she felt in necessary to remove the top from her pocket.

"You stop staring at it, Siman, or I'll make you sorry!" she whispered, and Siman wondered what greater capacity for sorrow she might think he had.

Mummy covered everything with the family's second blanket, and then hefted it all up as a bundle, which she slung over her shoulder.

"We're going," she said, and she stalked out without a backward look. The children, though, kept looking back as they trotted behind Mummy.

They passed an older man who was stooped over a clay oven, stirring in its pan some greens he'd found somewhere, perhaps discarded behind the nearest market. He appraised the three with growing concern, then sprang up to chase after them.

"Nephew, nephew," he said, gripping Siman's shoulder, "don't go that way. Take your mother this way. Please, nephew, that isn't the way for you today."

"What is it?" Mummy demanded. "Is Rachan hiding that way?"

"You don't want to know what's that way," the man said. "Nephew, please, go this way."

Igran took Mummy's hand firmly and said, "It doesn't matter which way we go." And she pulled Mummy along the path the man had said.

The boundaries of the slum were quite clearly demarked, for a settlement so haphazard; on one side was the lake, on the other the bog, and at its east tip the bog met the lake, so its access was only from the west, and that limit was abruptly imposed by a looming residential building of ten stories. It was called the Marika Towers for a reason known only to its developer; who Marika was or why the plural was applied to what would only tolerantly be seen as a single tower were questions unasked by slum people who passed there, almost all of whom couldn't read the embossed letters of its name, anyway. It was a strangely-located enclave of middle-class citizens, and its gate was guarded day and night by stern-faced young men armed with old Lee-Enfield rifles of bygone colonial days.

Beyond Marika Towers was a narrowing of the lake, and across the narrowing was a bridge that led to another world, one to which the two children had never been; it was a world of relative privilege, of the high apartment buildings for people of professions and prospects, for children who could attend school. They had seen this neighbourhood every day across the lake, of course, but it might have been on the moon for the sense of its accessibility.

And yet this is where Mummy led as she stalked from the slum. Igran and Siman exchanged frightened looks as they followed.

"They won't let us, Mummy," Igran protested, eventually.

"That's where we belong," Mummy insisted, pointing ahead. "We never belonged back there, and they all knew it as well as we did. If your Daddy were a better provider..."

They crossed the bridge and came to a little guardhouse by a lowered traffic barrier.

The uniformed guard who stepped from the guardhouse had a terrifying black metal rifle and a smile of utmost condescending amusement. He simply shook his head and pointed back to from where they had come. Siman thought that was all right.

"Delivery," Mummy said, shifting the pack on her back.

"What sort of delivery?" the guard asked.

"Pots," Mummy said. "Special order."

"Who for?"

"The doctor."

"Show me."

Mummy set the bundle down and drew out a pot. She was a fastidious housekeeper, and the pot shone like new.

The guard considered a moment, then said, "Okay, but only to the doctor's, and then straight out again."

He wouldn't bother to raise the bar for them, so they crawled beneath it and made their way.

Siman had always thought that it would be a clean place, unlike their fetid neighbourhoods, but it was soon apparent that these streets were littered with refuse and filth, as well, and there were open sewers of foul effluence along the side of every road, and the rising buildings, seeming to sparkle across the lake, were mouldy, rusting and crumbling. The buildings' balconies were all cluttered with drying laundry.

But there were real raised, paved footpaths, beside the high walls surrounding each building, and on those footpaths were actual electric streetlights, and beneath one of those streetlights, apparently arbitrarily, or by some process of conclusion at which one could only guess, Mummy rolled her little family like a mahogany pod rolling without direct purpose after falling from one of the street-lining trees.

She dumped down her pack and sat without a word, and when it became clear she wasn't merely pausing to rest, Igran and Siman sat down beside her.

Across the road from where they stopped was a building of flats they couldn't know was named Royal Towers. Siman examined the building closely for some time, as if anticipating it might be important. Igran, rather, wrapped her arms around her legs, set her cheek on one boney knee, and looked dolefully at the road in front of her, showing little interest in her new environs, didn't even raise her eyes when vehicles passed close to them.

After a long, silent time, she suddenly sprang up and skipped across the road to carefully pick up, between finger and thumb, a large, flat beetle that had been committed to its tiny but compelling objective somewhere farther down the road.

She returned to the footpath, sat again beside Siman, and set the beetle down before her, and used a long, dried seed pod to thwart its constant efforts to continue in its original direction. The beetle seemed beyond frustration, but persisted with patient determination to go its way as Igran repeatedly pushed it and blocked it. Siman looked on with limited interest, until he happened to spy a similar beetle walking with the same resolve in the opposite direction. He trotted to pick it up and bring it back. He set it down in confrontation of the first beetle.

"Okay, yours against mine," Igran said.

"It's not a game," Siman said. "I just want to see."

The beetles walked around each other every time the children positioned them to meet.

At one point, Igran plucked up her beetle, held it before her eyes and commanded "Stop being so boring!" and placed it down again, just to see it and Siman's beetle carefully bypass each other again.

She groaned and said "Hopeless! Boring!"

Siman, however, found it interesting, and he placed his beetle on the edge of the road to go its way. He peered down the road in the direction it went, failed to see anything attractive to boy or bug, but on it went, and he watched after it until perspective diminished it.

The children sat there for loyal hours, and Mummy fretted and clicked her tongue until she was suddenly seized by an idea.

"It's because you're both so dirty," she averred in final judgment. "That's why he thought we didn't belong here. He was noting you, not me."

She made them stand up and strip off their clothes, to Igran's bitter humiliation, as she fished in the bundle for a bottle of water, and then, with the water, she roughly washed them both. The children pictured unnumbered scornful and derisive faces at the windows of Royal Towers as they shivered in chill and dread.

Siman didn't remember having seen Igran naked before, and he made note of her.

"You turn your eyes away before I poke them out for you!" she said.

"Yours is different from mine," Siman said.

"Of course, it's different! I'm a girl, you're a boy!"

"Why does yours stick out?" he asked. "Mine doesn't."

"What sticks out?" she asked.

"Your bellybutton," he said. He looked down to his, neatly tucked away.

"It sticks out because I'm so hungry," she said.

Siman thought that out. In the brief glance he'd taken of it, he'd seen what appeared to be a crease across Igran's navel, and, in recollection, he could picture it as a pair of lips covering the teeth of a tiny mouth of a tummy that had sprung out in response to, and responsibility of, its hunger. He wondered if it might be able to speak, too. He inspected his own again, wondered just how hungry he'd have to be for it to become more assertive, less retiring.

As usual, Mummy pretty much ignored the children's conversation, treated it as something to which she had no attachment, even when it was of their umbilici.

They passed the day without any meal, and they slept that night within the illusive security of the streetlight's yellow circle, lying on one blanket and covered by the other. Igran and Siman slept in each other's arms, as they might have with Daddy, but Mummy never had invited such intimacy.

Before settling in beside Igran, Siman leant in to her belly and whispered, "I'm not food. Don't eat me."

"You are food," whispered either Igran or her bellybutton in answer. "You're nuts."

In the morning, Igran shook her brother awake.

"I'm not waiting anymore," she said. "Let's go get something to eat."

"Where?" he asked, sitting up.

"Where we find it."

In the branches of the small mahogany tree spreading above them, a crow perched, peering down at them, eyes glinting within its grey cowl, like a drab shade of a pirate princess, masked for BBC, Big Black Crow, and it followed the two, hopping or flapping between the branches of the line of trees, a familiar, perhaps, or an onyx talisman, or a flying foreshadowing, as they made their way along the footpath.

"What does it want?" Siman asked at one point.

"It thinks we're going to die," Igran said.

"Are we going to die?" he asked.

"Sorry, crow," she called up. "We're the ones who'll be eating today."

Siman looked up at it again, and it grinned wickedly down at him, more ravenous than a bellybutton.

They followed the sounds of traffic rolling awake, out of the residential area, and found themselves on Ortalt Avenue for the first time. Siman took Igran's arm and held on tightly as they wove through a press of purposeful pedestrians, shrunk away from blaring, spewing and snorting vehicles moving like a river of thick, slow sludge beside them. The street was lined with high, shining buildings of such aggressive intention, they made the Marika Towers look like a pile of their left-over scrap materials. They were emblazoned with bright, illuminated signs bearing messages transmitting nothing to the children but their urgency. Many of the buildings had ground level shops, welcoming to the wealthy, maybe, but forbidding to the children in their sleek, spare efficiency.

In time, they came to a side street, from which emanated blended smells of food, and their feet guided them down it automatically. On one side of the street, backing against a brick wall that enclosed a small park to which the two would never be admitted, were a number of food and tea stalls, some deep-frying various treats in wide, kerosene-fired pans of orange oil, others offering prepared foods. The best of the stalls sold baked goods of a sweet nature, some sugary loaves, some pies and a few fancy cakes. Between the stalls stood groups of men, all looking to the building across the street, a multi-storey mall catering to the fashion requirements of rich wives and daughters; a big sign on the building said 'Pink City' in scrawled handwriting, in English, which meant there were three reasons the children wouldn't have been able to read it.

Directly behind the mall was a tall tower of residential flats, and, on the footpath, to one side of the residence's iron gate, was a large drum of blue vinyl, and hanging from its top was a long-handled dipper. Igran, thirsty as well as hungry, led Siman to it, and, as expected, she found it filled with water, a generous gesture to passersby on a hot footpath in a stifling city.

She took the handle of the dipper, but, immediately, an armed guard appeared on the other side of the gate, and he barked them away.

"We're thirsty," she protested.

"Look for water back where you belong," he said. "That's not for you. You'll poison it."

She set the ladle back in its place, but stood staring at the guard for some time. His khaki uniform was worn and ill-fit; flat guards were cheap, and he was certainly much closer to Igran's caste than to that of the residents, but, on their turf, he identified more closely with them, and he watched Igran until she finally quit.

Igran led Siman up and down the extent of the food stalls, taking a sort of inventory. She understood why some of the men were eating the wares of the stalls, but she couldn't imagine why they all constantly attended to 'Pink City'. When she was sure she couldn't puzzle it out herself, she positioned Siman beside a palm tree, and went to a stall where a young man was frying shingaras. She had to pull her eyes from the pan and swallow hard before she could speak to him.

"Big brother, what are these men watching?"

The young man observed her without enthusiasm.

"Are you going to buy something?" he asked eventually.

"No, big brother, I don't think so."

"That's what I thought. If you have no money, then I have nothing for you," he said, swirling the bobbers in the pan.

"O, I have money," she said. "I'm surprised you can't answer my question, big brother. Of all the men on the street, you look by far the smartest to me. Was I fooled by your good looks?"

He raised his eyes from the pan, smiling slowly.

"You won't win a shingara from me that way," he said.

She smiled back at him.

"I don't know that I much like shingaras," she said. "Not yours, anyway. They're not as good-looking as you."

"My shingaras are as good as my looks," he laughed.

"Even that good? They can't be," she said.

"You can ask anyone here, they'll all tell you, my shingaras are the best to be had."

"But what good is the word of people who stand staring at a building like fools?"

The young man laughed again.

"The men who are dressed well are drivers," he said. "They're watching for their madams to come from the fashion shops across the way, so they can quickly get their cars from down the road. Those madams don't like being made to wait."

"O," said Igran. "And what about the others?"

"The ones who are dressed poorly are your fools. They stand here just to ogle pretty women coming and going."

"That's a strange thing to do. What about you, big brother? Do you watch the pretty women?"

"No, little sister; that would be as pointless as the way you watch my shingaras."

"Yes, big brother, you're right, and maybe, like you and your shingaras, they don't look so good up close, anyway."

She returned to her little brother.

"Am I pretty?" she demanded.

"Yes," he said.

"See if I'm as pretty as the women who come out of that door."

The entrance to the mall tower was elevated, up a set of wide stairs. When a group of elaborate women came out, they stopped at the top, didn't proceed down, but spoke to one another, ostensibly waiting for their drivers to draw up in expensive cars, but Igran was quite sure they were also posing and parading for the onlooking men, as well.

"Am I as pretty as them?" she asked Siman.

Siman studied them. "Their clothes are nicer."

"I'm not asking about their clothes."

"And they've got lots of gold things on."

"But am I as pretty as them?"

He examined his sister.

"Your arms are skinny. Theirs aren't," he said. He wasn't able to compare Igran's skinny legs, as the women's legs were hidden behind rich brocades. Some had bare midriffs, though, plump and rippled. "Their bellybuttons don't look hungry."

"Siman, answer sensibly. Is my face as pretty?"

Siman answered without hesitation. "O, your face is much prettier, Igran."

"That's what I thought," she said. "So why are all the men looking at those women and not at me?"

Siman didn't know why that would be, but he also didn't know why she'd think escaping their notice was a bad thing.

She turned her attention to the immediate material need, leant back against the palm tree, and surveyed the line of stalls. She raised her thumbnail to her teeth, and chewed lightly on it.

The best of them was the pastry shop, a proper enclosure, small but painted brightly. Its front was a large open window above a waist-high counter, and above the window space was a sign saying 'Sweets as Pie', written in English. It displayed its smaller treats on trays on the counter, and the pies and cakes on shelves along its back wall; it was clear that the stall, positioned as it was, directly across the road from the mall entrance stairway, was intended to sell to the mall clientele as much as those who awaited them, offering impulse purchases to self-indulgent people depleted by the rigours of shopping.

Behind the counter stood a middle-aged man wearing a striped, collared shirt; he was clean-shaven, and his thinning hair was neatly slicked back, and he looked across the road at the women in a manner other than the poorly-dressed oglers standing beside his booth.

Igran considered the man carefully for some time, then pushed herself up from the tree.

"You keep looking at me," she said to Siman. "When I signal, you come."

She went and stood directly in front of the counter, peering at the trays, putting her finger to her chin.

The man tolerated her a short while, then said "Move aside, girl. You'll obstruct my customers."

"I'm a customer," she said.

"I know a slum kitten when I see one. You're no customer. Customers buy things," he said, adding for clarity, "With money."

"I'm a customer," Igran protested. "I'm just waiting for my mummy. She said when she's finished across the road, she'll buy me a treat. I'm just trying to choose which one."

"Your mummy? Across the road? What's she doing, sweeping?"

"Buying things, of course," Igran said.

"Your mummy's never shopping there," the man derided. "Not in another lifetime. Now, move aside."

She moved slightly to one side.

"It's a hot day," she observed.

"Clear out," he snarled.

She shuffled another step or two, and the man behind the counter appeared set to step from his booth and chase her.

"Did I say my mummy?" she said suddenly, laughing. "I didn't mean my mummy. Goodness, my mummy couldn't buy anything here. I meant to say my madam. She's shopping across the road, and then she'll be buying me a sweet, she said."

She stepped back to the counter.

"Which one would you choose?" she asked. "You'd know which is best. You made them."

"I don't make them, I just sell them," he said. "Your madam is really across the road? You're her servant?"

"I wish she'd hurry up," Igran said. "Looking at these treats is making me hungry. Which one would you choose, uncle?"

The man sighed. "Don't ask me. I've diabetes."

Igran construed that he'd said a beeties would kill him.

"Then I won't choose a beeties, that's for sure. Which ones are they? Maybe you shouldn't even sell them."

"Your madam doesn't dress you well, even for a servant."

"She's very mean," Igran said.

"Then why is she buying you a treat?"

"She whipped me last night, and then she saw that it wasn't my fault, after all. So, she said she'll buy me a sweet today."

"I see. Just stand a bit to the side, there, while you're waiting," he said. He placed his hands on the counter in an attitude of protection.

"It's sure a hot day, uncle," she said.

"They're all hot days, this time of year, little niece," he said, sighing again.

"Whew, it's hot, though, uncle."

"Yes, it's hot."

"There's some water in that blue barrel across the road, by that gate," she said. "Do you see it? Let me bring you some water."

"I've got some water, little niece," he said, reaching under the counter and producing a small plastic bottle.

"But the man just finished filling the barrel; I saw him," she said. "His water won't be so warm. I'll bring you some, uncle, for your kindness."

"It's not necessary," the man said, but Igran had already started across the road.

When she approached the barrel, the guard again stepped to the gate.

"I told you before," he said sharply. "Stay away from that water. It's not for the likes of you."

"But I'm so thirsty," she said.

"Then go home to your slum and get some water there," he said, waving her away. "You shouldn't be here, anyway."

"The water at my slum is bad," she said.

"Whose fault is that? You'll turn this water bad, too." He stuck his hand through the bars and shooed her energetically.

"All right, if you won't let me drink, will you buy me a sweet at that stall over there?" she turned and motioned to the stall, and was pleased to see its keeper watching her.

"What?" the guard exclaimed.

"It's just over there, it's not far," she said, motioning to it again. "Please, please, please, buy me a sweet." She clasped her hands together in plea.

"You must be stupid," he said. "Thinking I'd buy a little scruff like you a sweet. Get away from here before I make you."

Igran burst out crying, ran back across the road to the pastry stall, sobbing and wiping her tears.

"O, uncle! It was so cruel, what the guard said about you!" she wailed. "He said the water wasn't for the likes of me, and I said fine, it wasn't for me, it was for my uncle at the sweets stall, and he's kind and good, and the guard said it's not for the likes of a lowly stall-keeper, either, and he called you a dirty dog; I told him, my uncle is kind and good, but he's not a coward, and if he wants a drink of your water, he'll come and take it, and you'll let him, if you know what's good for you. And he laughed and said he'd like to see the stupid old fool try. He was so cruel."

"He said that? A lowly guard lording it over me?" he said. "We'll see about that."

He stepped out the side doorway of the stall, clenching his fists. He took a few steps across the road, then turned to Igran.

"I've got my eye on you. Don't try anything."

"I'll watch your stall, uncle," she snuffled.

As soon as the man turned away from her, she signalled briskly for Siman to come to her. He trotted over, and as he did, she leant down to his ear and whispered, "Run back to Mummy, as fast as you can."

He gave a nod and started away, just as Igran shouted out "Stop, thief! Stop, thief!"

The stall-keeper spun at the far side of the road.

"Quickly! Quickly!" she cried, pointing to fleeing Siman. "He's getting away! He's getting away!"

The man took a moment to collect himself, then ran after Siman, and a number of bystanders joined the pursuit.

For a boy so young and small, Siman was unusually adept at rapidly snaking through crowds of people, and the stall-keeper and his party gained little on him as Siman raced around the corner and up Ortalt Avenue, his little legs churning on the uneven slabs and mounds of the footpath. It wasn't until a few blocks up, when there was an incidental thinning of pedestrians, that they were able to close the gap, and the stall-keeper slapped him sprawling to the ground.

"Oof!" Siman said, rolling over and sitting up. He rubbed his knee as the men bent and puffed over him, trying to regain their breath.

Eventually, the man had the wind to gasp out, "All right, where is it?"

"Where's what?" asked Siman, looking up in fear at the flushed men surrounding him.

"What you stole from my shop," the man panted.

"I didn't steal anything from your shop," Siman said.

"No? Then why were you running away from me?"

"I didn't know I was running away from you. I thought I was running to Mummy."

One of the men, wincing and wiping the sweat from his eyes, said, "He doesn't have anything with him. He must have thrown it away as he ran."

"I didn't see him throw anything," said another man, mopping his neck, and another man agreed.

The stall-keeper straightened.

"But the girl saw him," he insisted, but he paused, put his fingers to his lips. "The girl ... Lord Pakron preserve me."

He turned back down Ortalt, tried to run, but the heat, exertion and diabetes had left him exhausted, and he was reduced to an agitated shuffle.

The other men shifted about uncertainly. Siman got to his feet, and ran between them and away. They waved after him in humid dismissal.

Meanwhile, back at the pastry booth, Igran watched the men chasing after Siman in full hue and cry, then stepped through the doorway into the booth, assessing. She wished the keeper had identified the beeties she should avoid, but she used her best judgment to rank likeliness to be called 'beeties', and decided that the bottom of her list was a large, chocolate-frosted cake.

She slid it from the back shelf, where it occupied pride of place, atop a foam plastic sheet. It was quite weighty, but she thought she could carry it, skinny arms not preventing. She set it on the counter, then looked below it. It was still relatively early in the business day, and there weren't a lot of paltries divided in the slotted cash drawer, but she took what there was, and made her way along the opposite direction from Ortalt. At the young man's stall, his shingaras were cooling on a tray beside the deep-frying pan.

"What are you doing with that?" he asked.

"I just bought it for my dinner," she said. "But maybe I'll give your shingaras a try, after all, too. I thought they looked poor at first, but maybe I was wrong."

She set her cake down on the little bench by his table, a welcome relief for her arms, and pulled her wad of paltries from her pocket.

He opened a paper packet. "How many?"

"Hmm," she said, as though she could calculate.

He stood, poised.

"What am I thinking of?" she said suddenly, lifting her cake again. "This will be more than enough for me."

She carried on for a few blocks, then turned left in what she hoped was the right direction for Mummy; but, before long, she had to crouch on the footpath, balance the cake on her knees, in order to give her trembling arms some rest. As she squatted, a crow, the same crow, she thought, found her again, and swooped down to land on the top of a brick wall behind her, perching carefully between shards of broken glass set in the concrete crown to deter thieves like Igran.

She cast a fretful glance back up to the crow, assuming it meant to maraud.

"No cake for you!" she said. "Shoo!"

It cocked its head.

"Top!" it said.

"Pardon?" she asked.

"Top!" it repeated, thereby going from a familiar to overly familiar. "Top!"

"Shut up!" she said. "You don't know anything about it!"

It cocked its head to the other side, thinking, reconsidering. Then "Top! Top!" it said decisively.

"It wasn't my fault, I tell you! It was Fannel's, it was Malfren's!"

The crow shook its head at her. She grabbed a mahogany pod and flung it up at the bird. It calmly watched the projectile fly by, then repeated its accusation.

"I don't care what you say," Igran called up, but she stood before she was much rested and stalked away.

It took her some time, wrong turns and fruitless explorations to find the road on which Mummy was camped, by which time her arms were noodles, and she was quite incapable of casting anything but aspersions at the following crow.

She set the cake down on the footpath beside where Mummy sat on her haunches; Mummy regarded the cake as though it were of a daily delivery.

"Didn't Siman get back?" Igran asked.

"Who?" Mummy asked.

Igran sighed, and started back along their first route of the morning.

The crow glided silently into the mahogany tree over Mummy's head, and looked down on her.

"Feduk," it said. "Feduk, Feduk."

"Who?" Mummy asked.

Igran eventually came upon Siman, who was following the proper route, just limping along it slowly.

"What happened to you?" she asked.

"Some men knocked me down," he said. "They thought I stole something."

"I wonder why they thought that."

"You do? I don't."

She leant down to inspect his knee. It was scraped raw, and tiny stones were embedded in it. She spit on it and gave it a rub.

When they returned to Mummy, she had carved up the cake with a wooden spatula. None of them would have understood the frosted message on its top, anyway: Happy Birthday, none of which had any pertinence to them. Theirs was a very quiet festival, eating it.

Mummy had had a practice of hanging items in plastic mesh bags from the bamboo rafters of their slum shed, and she did something similar with the remainder of the cake, forming it into a brown ball, and suspending it in a bag from the lower branch of the nearest mahogany tree.

That night, in the smoke, they settled down to sleep at the same arbitrary spot on the footpath, seemingly ordered according to size, but not actually; Mummy, at a moment as random as the spot, merely chose to lie down and spread the cloth over herself --- "Sleep," she said --- and then Igran, after a wait adequate to indicate she wasn't doing as she'd been told, chose to lie down and pull the cloth over herself, too, and then Siman followed, and he didn't care how that appeared. He was tired, his knee was sore, and his head and belly were failing to find consensus on the qualities of the cake.

Siman's sleep was fitful, as his stomach made a more compelling case, and his mind was troubled by attempted accommodations, so when, sometime in the night, he half-opened his eyes to observe, by the yellow light of the street lamp, two big grey rats nearby, springing upward in efforts to reach the cake bag, the sight slipped without a splash and unsurprisingly into the choppy current of his dreams.

One after the other, the rats leapt up at the bottom of the bag, but fell short each time; they seemed to settle into a sequential rhythm of sorts, and, together, they impressed fretful, sleepy Siman as a toy almost as troubling as a wooden top.

He closed his eyes, and the vision shimmered into a little dream in which rats leapt in his stomach, but he was roused by excited whistles and squeaks, opened his eyes to see that one of the rats was hanging by its teeth from the bottom of the bag, possibly snagged on one of the thin plastic strands, and it was wriggling and flailing, trying to climb higher. The other rat was poised below, then sprang up, gripped the hanging rat's hind leg in its teeth; the upper rat reacted ill, kicked frantically at the lower with its free hind leg, and they contorted and squeaked, tails twitching stiffly.

Siman tried to raise his head to see more accurately, but it swam, so he closed his eyes and let his mind subside, but then his curiosity roused him again, and he opened his eyes in time to see that either the upper rat's teeth or the filament on which they were snagged let go, and the two rats fell to the footpath. The focus of the lower rat appeared to have shifted from the cake in the bag, though, and it didn't release its toothhold on the upper rat's leg, so the first rat wriggled around to sink its teeth into the second rat's hind leg, so that they formed a circular argument without a premise. And thus they remained, spinning and squeaking, but refusing to yield.

Their twists carried them closer to the edge of the footpath, toward the road, until, from the black above, a crow swooped down to land beside them; it cocked its head as if assessing a puzzle, then after a further moment's consideration, it pecked sharply at each rat in turn; the rats squealed in muffled protest, but wouldn't let go of each other.

"Fed up. Fed up," the crow interjected. "Fed up."

"What?" asked Siman.

In answer, the crow pecked several times more, and its grey cowl became flecked with red spray, but the rats were relentless. Then it closed its beak on a tail, and flung the rat ball into the street, hopping after it.

Siman closed his eyes and drifted away into dyspeptic dismay.

When he surfaced again, it was to a soft clattering, and he saw a little goat standing beside him, and beside that was another little goat that perched, its forehooves on the shoulder of the first, and by that means it was reaching high enough to nibble cake through the mesh bag; and, after it had eaten a while, the higher goat stepped down and positioned itself under the bag, and the other set its forehooves on its shoulder, and so they both got a little meal, and then they trotted away together.

Siman thought the little episode of greater value than the cake that was lost. He wondered, though, if the cake would exact the same revenge on the goats as it did on him. He slipped back into sleep to dream of beetles that won't fight and rats that won't stop and little goats gaining the prize that might poison them and crow-shaped cake punishing errors.

In the morning, he awoke to find his sister bent by the roadside, examining something.

"Yuck," she said with distaste, but she clearly meant it as an invitation to Siman to come and look, too.

Mummy still slept beneath the cloth.

The subject of Igran's scrutiny was the rat ball, or what remained of it. The rat jaws were still latched onto the other's hind legs, but considerable amounts of flesh were absent. The fur on what was left was wet and spikey, dark brown against livid red.

"We need to cover this up before Mummy decides it's our breakfast," Igran said.

Siman, still quite queasy, started to look away, but his eye was arrested by the appearance of one hind paw: it was pink, curled slightly in a gentle elegance denied it in life, and, somehow, seemed to express a certain innocence, and mirrored the form of Daddy's easy smile. Siman watched it a while, wondering how a rat might assume in its death what Daddy had lost in his.

Igran collected some mahogany hulls and other scraps of stuff, and concealed the carcasses beneath them.

"Now to get some food for today," she said.

"Not the same food," Siman moaned.

"I thought you liked it."

"My mouth liked it, but my tummy didn't," he said.

"Oh-oh," she said, putting her hand to her mouth. "Beeties."

"Beeties? What's beeties? Is it bad?"

"Very bad," she said. "Beeties will kill you. That must be what we ate."

"Why did you feed me beeties?" he asked.

"Why does that man at the stall even sell beeties? It's his fault, not mine."

"Will Mummy and you die, too?"

"I feel fine," Igran said, taking quick stock. "Some people are tougher than beeties."

"Not me," said Siman. "When will I die?"

Igran referred to her full experience.

"Well, first you'll get a lot less hair on your head," she said. "And your nose will get big and funny."

She came and inspected his scalp.

"No, it looks like it's all still there," she said judiciously.

"What about my nose?"

"Well, it looks funny," she said, wiggling it a bit, "but just in the way it always looks funny. I think maybe you're tougher than beeties, too. I didn't think you were tougher than anything."

"Neither did I," he said. "When will I start feeling better?" He was fearful that, even if it didn't kill him, the sting of beeties hits a boy forever.

"Maybe soon," she said. "Maybe not so soon."

"What about little goats? Are they tougher than beeties?"

"Nothing can kill a goat," she said firmly, although that this is incorrect would serve a ploy of hers some years later.

Siman was more relieved over the goats' probable survival than he was over his own.

Igran went and poked Mummy a couple of times with her toe.

"Are you sick?"

Mummy sat up and wiped her face.

"Are you sick?" Igran repeated.

"I'm tired," Mummy sighed. "He wouldn't be quiet all night."

"Well, he was feeling sick," Igran said.

"Not sick," Mummy said. "Just cruel."

"I didn't mean to be cruel. I thought I was quiet," Siman said.

"What's the worst thing you could say to someone who sells street food?" Igran asked Mummy.

Mummy considered for a moment without asking the purpose of the question.

"You could say his wife's ugly," she said.

"No, no, I mean about his food. What's the worst thing you could say about his food? Besides it being beeties, I mean."

"Well, Daddy said some people got in trouble for cooking badly, somehow," Mummy offered.

"O, yes," Siman said. He remembered Daddy laughing and shaking his head over a report he'd heard at his barber chair. "They were frying in bad oil, and they got in trouble. Old engine oil."

"What's that?" Igran asked.

"I don't know, but Daddy thought it wasn't good."

"Mummy, what's old engine oil?" Igran asked.

"Why are you tormenting me with these questions? Can't you see I'm tired?" She turned and laid herself down again.

"I guess it's like mustard oil," Siman suggested, "but I guess you squeeze it out of old engines."

"So, engines are like mustards?"

"I guess so. I've never seen a mustard. Only its oil."

Igran looked dubious, but she took her brother by the shoulder and guided him back through the streets to the footpath stalls opposite the Pink City Mall.

They were too early in the morning. The stall-keepers were there, but only starting their preparations, not offering cooked food for sale. Igran led her brother back to a side street to wait, and they crouched at the roadside.

"What are you going to do?" he asked.

"You'll see," she said lightly. "Nothing bad."

Across the road was an old man, dressed against the morning chill in a tattered sweater, with a scarf wrapped around his head like a kerchief. He bent before the rubble of a demolished brick fence, the opposite ends of which still stood, forming Igran's sly grin; the old man seemed to be sorting through the broken bits of brick and concrete, his pelvis sharply delineated through his thin cotton lunghi as he bent. Slowly, he lifted one chunk in one gnarled hand, then, after some seconds, another in the other, and he carried them five or six paces, to a clear space marginally closer to the road, and dropped them, then straightened and returned to the first pile to do the same again, and then again, and then again, sometimes setting chunks aside, out of his way, to select, by some criteria beyond Siman's imagination, a chunk more appropriate to the moment. Siman watched woefully, transfixed, as one pile shrunk and the other grew.

He was glad when Igran finally broke the spell, standing and telling him to follow. She led him back to the market street, and down to a point across the street from the man selling round shingaras, flat samosas, and pakoras.

"Wait here, but come as soon as I call you," she instructed.

"O, no!" he protested. "Not again! It's not right."

"Don't be a sissy, Siman. We have to eat, haven't we?"

Siman wasn't sure that they had to eat, not if that amounted to no better design than moving brick rubble.

Igran hopped across the road, and positioned herself squarely before the shingara man.

"Hello again, big brother," she said.

"Good morning, little sister," he said. "Come to refuse my good food again?"

"I'm just checking, because your shingaras didn't look so bad to me when I saw them yesterday."

"And how do they look today?"

"Well, I still don't see what's so bad about them," she said. "I don't see anything the matter with them."

"Well, of course, little sister. Why would there be anything the matter with them? They're the best shingaras you've never bought."

She peered into his smoking kettle of oil.

"That doesn't look like old engine oil to me," she said.

"What are you talking about, old engine oil?" he demanded.

"The new shingara man, set up around the corner; he's telling everyone you cook in old engine oil; but these don't look so bad to me..."

"What new shingara man?"

"The one set up around the corner; I told him, my big brother wouldn't cook in old engine oil, he doesn't even have any old engines. You don't have any old engines, do you?"

"He said ---?"

"Don't worry, big brother, I don't believe him, even if everyone else he's telling does...."

"He's telling everyone ---?"

"I guess you're not selling much today, are you? Too bad...."

"Around which corner?" the man growled.

"Down there and that way," Igran said, pointing.

The man reached under his counter, brought up a cudgel, and stepped out from behind.

"I'll watch your stall for you," Igran said. "Don't worry."

The man stalked down the road, and Igran motioned urgently to Siman.

Siman trotted across quickly, but before Igran could speak, he said "Run."

"What?" she said.

"Run," he repeated, then raised his voice to a hue and cry "Stop, thief! Help! Thief!"

Down the road, the shingara man stopped and turned.

"Just you wait!" Igran hissed as she flew away.

The shingara man was still collecting himself as Igran zipped away, but soon bolted after her, cudgel held high.

Igran was a little gazelle, Siman knew , and he wasn't much worried about her, but, with his inculcated sympathy for anyone who, like Daddy, tried to eke a livelihood from a roadside, he thought perhaps he should wait at the shingara counter until the owner returned. He didn't think he'd be able to do anything more than raise another alarm, should anyone try to exploit the owner's absence, but that might be enough, so he moved behind the counter and tried to seem a stern guardian.

Before long, a nicely dressed man came to the counter.

"Where's Dreffel?" he asked.

"He's away," Siman said, and he tried to cough his throat clear.

"Hm," he said, assessing the goodies stacked on the counter. "These are from this morning?"

"Yessir," Siman said.

"Not yesterday's, reheated?"

"Nossir, they're new."

"Okay, I'll have ten shingaras and ten pakoras."

"O," said Siman, "um… he'll be back soon, maybe."

"I'm in a hurry, boy," the man said. "Ten each, please, shingaras and pakoras."

Siman gaped a moment, then found a starting point by seeing a stack of paper bags on a slot shelf beneath the counter. He pulled out a bag and put a shingara in it, but then stopped, not knowing how many more than one ten was.

"And nine more," the man said.

Siman reckoned that nine more was certainly more than one more, so he put two more into the bag.

"And now seven more," the man said.

Siman added two more.

"Here, let me," the man said, taking the bag. "Watch." He added five more, counting as he did.

"That's ten?" Siman asked.

"Yes, son, that's ten. Now we'll count out ten pakoras, as you put them in another bag, all right?"

They did that, and Siman was feeling a bit accomplished until he met the obstacle of the money to be paid.

"Money now, please, sir," he said simply.

"How much?"

Siman sighed and looked down to the counter, but then he raised his eyes to those of the man.

"Please, sir, don't cheat."

The man chuckled and said "I'm sorry, little brother. I was teasing you. I buy these here every day, and it's ten paltries for a shingara and seven paltries for a pakora; but you don't know what that would come to, do you?"

"I don't like being stupid, sir. I'm not always lazy, but I'm always stupid."

"No, I didn't mean you to think you're stupid, son. You haven't had a chance to learn yet, have you? It comes to one hundred and seventy paltries."

"Does it?"

"Honestly." The man pulled a worn wallet from his back pocket, and counted out the paltry notes. "How old are you, son?"

"What do you mean?" Siman asked.

"I mean, how long have you been alive?"

Siman blinked. "I wasn't alive?"

The man sighed and shook his head, and, as he started away, he turned back to say "Tell your father you should be in school, not working in a market."

Siman, with no knowledge of what a school is, no work in a market, and no father to tell, put the paltries on the shelf and hoped nobody else would want to buy anything. He stared at the shingaras a while, and wondered why he went from nausea to hunger directly, with no neutral relief between.

In time, the stall-keeper returned, flushed and furious, jerked his head up at the sight of Siman behind the counter, and then scanned his inventory.

"She didn't get away with all that!" he cried.

"No, a man bought them. She didn't get any," Siman said, and he reached under the counter and then held the money out to the stall-keeper.

"A man bought them? And he put the money there?" he asked, taking the notes.

"I put it there," Siman said. "He was honest."

"And you, too," the man said.

Siman shifted out from the stall.

"Wait," the man said. "Would you like a shingara?"

"I don't have money," Siman said.

"No, from me, to say thanks for watching the stall. Take one."

"No," Siman said. "One shingara would make me unhappy."

"How so?"

"If I ate a shingara, then Mummy and Igran would be hungry, and I'd be unhappy. If I gave it to Mummy, Igran would be hungry and maybe mad, and I'd be hungry and unhappy, and if I gave it to Igran, Mummy would cry, and then I'd be unhappy."

"Okay, then, how many shingaras would make you happy?"

"If Mummy and Igran had shingaras, I'd be hungry, but I might be happy, too."

"But three would make you even happier."

Siman thought he'd bluff his way through this confusing world of numbers. "Yes," he said.

"But losing three shingaras would make me unhappy."

"Oh," said Siman.

"Okay, kid," the man said. "No reason all four of us should be unhappy."

He put three shingaras in a packet and handed it to Siman.

"Sometimes I could use some help around here," the man said, "in exchange for shingaras, maybe. Come check with me now and then."

"I should be in school, not working in a market," Siman said to the man, for want of a father.

The man snorted. "Beggar atop an elephant. Good luck!"

As Siman neared Mummy's footpath camp, Igran ambushed him, her little fists clenched, but he defended himself by waving the bag in front of her nose, as a matador might a cape before a charging bull. She hesitated, then sniffed deeply.

"How did you get those? Did you steal them?"

"No," he said.

"Then how did you get them?"

"I don't know. It just happened."

She took the packet and peered in.

"These don't just happen," she said. "There may be hope for you, yet."

The shingaras weren't very large, so the three ate them slowly and carefully.

"You know, Siman stole these," Igran said to Mummy.

"No, I didn't," Siman said.

"Not too bad for a first try," said Igran, "but you should have taken more."

"Thank Pakron, your father never saw his son a thief," Mummy said severely, but her shame didn't affect her appetite.

Siman asked Mummy what school is, and she told him it's a place where rich people put their children.

"A man said I should be in school," Siman said.

"Did he say how you should pay for it?" Mummy asked with a scoff.

"He said I should be in school and shouldn't work in a market."

"Sounds like either one would cut into your valuable stealing time," said Igran, "so they're both no good."

That thought spurred her; there's only so much sustenance from a single shingara, and she called for Siman to follow her. Together, they roamed the streets, directionless, until they heard, from some distance, a singsong voice rising above the normal din.

"Listen," Igran said, stopping a moment. "He says he's selling chickens."

"Chickens?"

"Come on," she said, starting away at a trot.

They traced the call to the next street over, found a very poor-looking man who was wearing a very peculiar hat comprised of a shallow, wide, woven basket balanced atop his head, and in the basket sat several chickens that peered over its rim and bounced and swayed as the man walked along.

"Chickens! Good chickens!" he sang in a two-note refrain, repeating it every few paces. He was singing to the windows of the buildings of flats that rose on either side of the road.

"Mmm, chicken," Igran said as they caught up to the man, falling into step a short distance behind him.

"Those birds, you mean?" Siman asked. "What are they for?"

"For eating," she said. "Chicken's good to eat."

They didn't look good to Siman. He peered up at them as they peered down at him; their bobbing heads seemed those of tiny little old women bitterly disapproving of him. From time to time, one of them, angry-eyed, would open its sneering beak just enough ask a short question about why-y-y, why-y-y, why-y-y Siman chose to be as displeasing as he was.

"When did you eat a chicken?" Siman asked.

"Rachan's wedding feast," she said. "Now, be quiet and let me think."

"Rachan asked you to her wedding feast?"

"No, she didn't ask me. Let me think."

She put her thumb to her lip as they went along behind the chicken hawker. She studied the basket intently, as Siman wondered if her thumb was necessary to her scheming, if a capricious thumb accident might usher them into a more honourable life.

In time, she grabbed Siman by the shoulder of his tee-shirt and pulled him along a side road, then up a road parallel to the first.

"Hurry, hurry! Faster!" she said.

After they scampered two blocks up, she yanked him along another side road back to the road on which they'd come upon the chicken man.

Siman looked back down the road, saw the basket bonnet some way behind them.

"Don't look there," Igran said, pulling him into the middle of the road. "Look up."

And she looked up, herself, directly up, shielding her eyes. Siman looked up, as well, but all he saw was the normal smog blanket.

"I don't see anything," he said.

"Yes, you do. Keep looking."

A rickshaw wallah wheeled up to them, and he paused, set a foot on the ground, and looked up, too; then two young boys in school uniforms joined them.

"What is it?" asked one boy, craning his neck.

"Do you see it? Wow. Do you see it?" Igran asked, cupping her eyes.

The driver of a car honked at them, but no one moved, and then the driver stopped, got out, and looked up.

"Where is it?" asked the other boy.

"Straight up," Igran said. "Don't you see it?"

"Maybe," said the wallah.

"It just went behind that little cloud, there. Wait a minute."

"What is it?" the driver asked.

"That's what I'd like to know," Igran said.

By the time the chicken man came up to them, the knot had grown by a few more drivers, all straining upward.

"So weird," Igran said.

"I'm scared," said a boy.

"So am I," Igran agreed.

"What is it?" a driver asked again.

The chicken man started to raise his eyes, but then remembered himself. He carefully set his basket on the road, cupped his hands over his eyes and looked upward.

"O! Look, look, look!" Igran urged, even as she stepped backward out of the group. "There! There! I think it's --- I think it's ---"

"What? What?" cried the boy.

"I think it's time to go!" Igran squealed, zipping away, her hand swooping down to grab a chicken by its neck as she went. She ran off, laughing, her arm straight out, the chicken flapping wildly.

Siman sighed and dropped his head, as the others tried to make sense.

"I think I see it," one boy said, whose attention remained up where Igran had directed.

The chicken man, though, watched her flee, then sat down beside his basket, slumped, his face in his hands. Siman couldn't discern if he was crying or merely muttering morosely. It occurred to Siman that, just maybe, the man had hoped for a good day's business, that he might buy his young son some marbles on the way home, and Siman didn't want to think of that, so he slipped away, even as the group hesitated to disband and took last upward glances.

In the course of making his way back to Mummy, Igran suddenly appeared beside him, still holding the chicken at arms length.

"Here, you take this stupid bird awhile. Its flapping is killing my arm."

The chicken regarded Siman with the same censure as before. Still, without a word, he took the bird in both hands, but he threw it up into the air. It flapped, then just fell to the roadway.

"What's the matter with you?" Igran cried.

"What's the matter with it?" Siman asked. "Why didn't it fly away?"

"Its wings are tired from beating at me," Igran said.

"Maybe it's sick," Siman said, bending down to look closely, wondering if its disgust was based on some malaise other than what his appearance generated, after all. The chicken blinked and continued to look at him in a way that rice and lentils never had. "I don't want to eat it if it's sick."

"You mean you only want to eat it if it flies away?"

SIman thought a moment. "Yes."

"It's not sick. Bring it along."

He lifted it in both hands, and it put up only token resistance to his method. Igran took the bird back from him, though, as they approached Mummy, who was squatting on the footpath and gesturing mysteriously.

"Look what I got," Igran said to her, tossing it to the footpath.

Mummy blinked at the chicken as it blinked at her.

"What's that for?"

"It's for you to cook for our dinner, of course."

Mummy poked at it cautiously.

"How?" she asked.

"Cook it in a curry," Igran said.

"We don't have what we need for a curry," Mummy said. "Get me some masala, then."

"Well, then, don't cook it in a curry, just cook it. I'm not going to eat it raw."

Siman wished they'd stop speaking about cooking and eating the chicken while it could hear every word they said.

"You have to take the feathers off, first," Mummy said. "That's a child's job."

"How?" Igran asked.

"You just pull them off. We can't eat feathers, can we?"

Igran studied the chicken a moment.

"That's a boy's job," she concluded. "Pull them off, Siman."

Siman reached down to the feathers on the back and gave an experimental little tug. The chicken swivelled its head around and pecked his hand, rat-a-tat, as a crow would interlocking rats.

"I don't think that's a boy's job," he said, rubbing his hand.

"Yes, it's always a boy's job," Igran said quickly. "That's how it is."

Siman reached down cautiously again, but the chicken was ready for him, and pecked wickedly at him even before he put finger to feather. Siman straightened and stuck his hand behind his back, not that the bird gave any evidence of active pursuit; it sat where it was, beak slightly opened and tongue lifted, and flicked its head, as though Siman's sweat had dripped onto it.

"It won't let me," he said.

"Make it do what you want," Igran said, but she wasn't able to make him do what she wanted.

Mummy watched the chicken a while, and then offered up "I think you have to kill it first, then pull off the feathers. That would be the way."

The chicken regarded Siman with the same recrimination.

"No. I don't want to kill it," he said.

Igran looked down at the bird and wiggled her toes in the grit.

"It never did anything bad to me," Siman said.

"Well, it poked your hand, and flapped my arm," Igran suggested. "That wasn't so good."

"That's not enough for me to kill it."

"I'm hungry," Mummy said.

Igran spun on her. "Then get yourself some food."

"I would, if I weren't so busy taking care of useless children," Mummy said.

Siman decided on the spur to go for a little run, but, after starting, he soon decided that a longer one would be better, best with his eyes closed, so that, when he finally opened them again, he wouldn't know where he was, wouldn't know how to return.

He closed his eyes, but the footpath was so heaved and uneven underfoot, and so many other people were on it, he quickly reconsidered, compromised to the extent of opening his eyes just a little, about as much as a defensive chicken beak, and he kept going, knee aching and chest quaking, until he felt a hand grip his shoulder hard.

"Wait up," Igran gasped.

He yielded to her pull, and stopped dead.

"Where are you going?" she asked.

"Nowhere," he said, but that wasn't really true; he was trying to go nowhere, but he wasn't getting there.

Igran panted and wiped her forehead.

"I don't want to kill the chicken," Siman said.

"I know. I don't want to, either," she said. "I didn't think about the killing part when I grabbed it. It's mean, but it didn't hurt us very badly, and I think you're right: we should only kill the things that really hurt us."

"Is that what I said?" Siman asked.

"You're right. So, we should put the chicken in a tree or something until it rests up enough to fly away."

"Okay."

"But that means we have to find something else to eat, something we don't have to kill."

They wandered around until they came upon an extensive indoor market. Perhaps they were guided by their noses, for the market was redolent with the reek of old fish and rotten mutton; hygiene wasn't its watchword, it was plain, but it wasn't established for the custom of the wealthier people whose flats surrounded it, but for their servants, their cooks and housekeepers, most of whom came from stinky and filthy neighbourhoods, themselves, and, presumably, had higher tolerance for merchants' neglect of rubbish aisles and passageways.

Igran led Siman around, sniffing by the reddening pigeon and chicken carcasses set out on metal tables, past the astounded goat heads, past shallow water pans of flapping fish, to the booths selling produce. All of them were set up the same way: fruit and vegetables were carefully stacked on counters in high, mathematical pyramids, behind which the merchant sat on a raised platform, imperious in his station, surveying the passersby and the two or three poor boys he employed to exhort possible customers and to guard his wares. The boys quite clearly conducted themselves with a pride and swagger as they extolled their produce with polished patter and selected whatever items of it a customer requested. Then the merchant would extend down to the customer a small, flat basket affixed to a long wooden pole, that to receive the customer's payment. If change was required, the merchant would make it, and send it by basket back down to the customer. The boys in the aisles never touched the money.

Igran watched these operations awhile, then focussed on a booth that had only one boy patrolling the aisle before it.

"When was the last time you had an apple?" she asked Siman.

"I don't know," he said.

"Okay, get ready," she said.

"Igran, use your money," he said.

"There you go again, Siman," she said. "Sometimes you seem to say something smart, but then you go back to being all stupid again. If I use my money, I won't have any, will I?"

"I don't want to steal anymore."

"You're looking at this all wrong, as usual. Didn't you say we shouldn't kill things that never hurt us? And didn't I agree with you? Well, if we don't eat, we'll die, won't we?"

"Will we?"

"Yes, we will die. So, these people are trying to kill us by keeping food from us. And did we ever hurt them?"

"No," Siman said.

"No, we never hurt them at all, not even a little bit, so they shouldn't try to kill us, should they?"

"No," Siman admitted.

"So, it isn't wrong for us to stop them from killing us. You don't blame that chicken for poking you, do you?"

"No."

"Then, why do you blame me?"

"That man with the chicken hat looked unhappy..."

"Of course, he was unhappy. He wanted to starve us, and we didn't let him. I'm glad he was unhappy. He got what he deserved."

Something of Igran's argument seemed skewed to Siman, but he couldn't figure out what, and he didn't need to be convinced of Igran's superior brainpower, which was a given understood by all, so he fell silent.

"Be ready," she said, stepping along to her chosen booth.

The attendant boy instinctively stepped between Igran and the stacks, spreading his arms to shepherd her along the passage.

"My madam sent me to buy stuff," Igran said up over the boy's shoulder, to the lord on high.

"Show me your money," he said.

Igran produced her wad of bakeshop paltries, and the merchant nodded to his assistant.

"We'll need a bag," Igran said. "My madam wants a lot of stuff."

The boy took a plastic mesh bag and set about filling it with items Igran specified at random --- that funny white thing, that round green thing --- until the bag was heavy and nearly full.

"O, and some apples," she said.

"How many?" the boy asked, selecting one from the top of the apple pyramid.

"I think these ones look better," she said, reaching for some of the bottom rank.

"Stop!" cried the merchant and boy in unison.

"What?" asked Igran, scooping up an armload.

The ranks of apples above did what we might expect them to do, rolling in a cascade to the floor below. The boy, still holding the bag, watched helplessly as Igran, on the other side of the red tide, made off with her windfalls. Nearby shop-boys were too arrested by the sight to pay much attention the girl slipping by them.

Siman looked on, overwhelmed not only by his sister's escapade, but also by how much he didn't know about everything; he had had no information, for instance, about what would happen to a stack of apples if you pulled out the bottom ones, not as Igran and the booth boy clearly knew, and he slumped under the enormity of his ignorance.

A little swirl in his fog suggested to him that, perhaps, he should help pick up the fallen apples that the booth boy was just bending to collect. The boy misconstrued his intentions, though, thought Siman a gleaning opportunist, and snatched the apples from him, as the merchant above sent strewn deprecations. Then a nearby merchant identified Siman as having been in the company of the chaos girl, so Siman scooted.

Once again, Igran was waiting for him, unseen, along the way, and she appeared suddenly, cradling five apples to her chest. She told him to take two of them.

"I don't think they want us back in that market again," he said.

"I don't think so," she agreed, and she thought a while as they walked. "We're going to run out of places we can go. We need a better plan."

When they returned to Mummy, they found her crouched at the roadside, poking at a small, smudgy fire, over which she'd set up an arrangement of sticks, and atop those sticks was propped another stick skewering the carcass of the chicken. The chicken head sat upright in a red pool on the footpath. It stared without mercy at Siman.

"You killed the chicken?" Igran asked.

"Well, I had to kill it," Mummy said. "It kept saying 'Feduk' at me."

It was clear that Mummy had been impatient or incapable with the process of plucking; wherever the skin of the bird hadn't been ripped off, it was still covered in feathers; much of the fluff was singed away, but the shafts remained. As food, the chicken looked like something from which a starving dog would worriedly back away, and the fire below it reeked.

"That stuff she's burning...," Siman asked Igran, "isn't that the pile you made this morning?"

Igran wrinkled her nose and nodded.

"Well, tell her," Siman said.

Igran gave her head a little shake and looked on with curiosity.

But accusations flew at Siman from the chicken head.

"Mummy, you're cooking with rats," he said.

Mummy stopped stoking and inspected the chicken. "No, it's a bird," she said.

"You're burning rats to cook the chicken," Igran said. "That's a pile of dead rats."

"Wicked girl, why are you saying that?" Mummy said. "You want it all for yourself, is that it, selfish girl? You think I'm as easily fooled as that?"

Igran smiled. "Mummy, you can have it all. Your wicked children will only get apples, because we're so wicked."

"Well, I'll still share with you," Mummy said patiently.

"No, no, we haven't learned our lesson. We must be punished. Only apples for us. That will teach us, all right."

When the skewer stick burnt through and the chicken fell into the ash and embers, Mummy fished it out with her knife, but by doing so, she spread out the smoldering pile, and exposed the charred rat ball; a new wave of stench revealed rot to the corpse, perhaps. Siman hoped that would be the end of it, but Mummy poked at the redolent rodents a bit, took a quick sidelong glance at her daughter, then took the chicken and hacked it apart with the knife, with real difficulty. She tossed a leg to Siman, who let it fall to the ground, and a wing to Igran, who did likewise; then Mummy started to gnaw at the breast.

Siman looked at his rat-smoked, red and feathered leg, and pushed it away from himself with his toe. Igran watched him and laughed. They turned their attention to Mummy, who was chewing gamely on a strip of red elastic flesh she'd managed to tear off.

"Mmmm, yummy!" Igran said, and she laughed again.

Siman looked away, scanned the Royal Towers across the road. He looked back, though, when he heard Mummy's violent capitulating spits and retching clearings of her throat, with evoked fresh peals of laughter from Igran.

"You brought a bad chicken!" Mummy said around her fingers, which were wiping inside her mouth for any remnants. "Why didn't you bring a good chicken?"

She seemed to have ingested some fowl spirit despite her expulsion, for her expression was awfully similar to that of the chicken head. When she, in answer to Igran's laughter, let out some sounds rather like clucks and gesticulated in motions rather like flapping, Siman became alarmed.

"Igran, she's turning chicken!" he said.

"Turning chicken!" Igran clapped. "O, Mummy, lay some eggs!"

Mummy rose from her squat, chicken held high, and she flung it at Igran, who, still laughing, rolled out of its trajectory. Then Mummy reached down for the knife, raised her hand again.

Igran stopped laughing.

"Go on, Mummy," she said quietly. "I dare you."

"Wait! Wait!" Siman thawed from his frozen moment, and he sprang between the two. "Stop, stop."

He reached up to grip Mummy's arm, to pull down her hand. She regarded him as though he were unknown to her.

"Please, Mummy," he said.

Mummy resisted his pull, held her hand up still, but, in another few seconds, she opened it, and the knife fell to the ground. She rubbed her face, top to bottom, then raised her chin and assumed her proud look. She eyed Igran evenly.

"You're right, Siman," Igran said. "She turned chicken."

"What are you trying to make me do?" Mummy asked. "I won't let you."

Mummy squatted down again, and Siman brought her an apple. She ate it as if it were poor compensation for all she'd been made to suffer.

"Don't choke on the bad apples I brought you," Igran said.

"Why are you so cruel?" Mummy asked.

The two females fell into silent apple rumination, wrought to the core, perhaps.

Siman bit into one, too, and found it rather too bright and sweet for his mood, but the taste was also too appealing to stop, and its smell was, possibly, as directly opposite that of burning rat as his world could provide.

Igran looked over to him in time, and told him not to eat the middle.

"Why not?"

"Because those are the seeds. Daddy said if you eat them, an apple tree will grow in your belly."

"Yes, it's true," Mummy confirmed. "Your father knew that much, anyway."

Siman thought about it as he chewed.

"Apples make apple trees?" he asked.

"Yes."

"Do apple trees make apples?"

"No, lizards make apples," she said.

Siman thought more.

"How?" he asked.

"Siman, don't be silly. Of course, apple trees make apples."

Siman fumbled toward the hopeful fallacy of the circle of life, Ouroboros shoving its tale down his throat, no more viable, in reality, than two rats locked in their circle of lice.

"Well, then, wouldn't it be good to have an apple tree in your belly? Then you'd always be eating apples, wouldn't you?"

"Siman, think about how big an apple tree is."

"How big is it?"

"Well, it's a tree, isn't it?" she exclaimed. "Look at these trees, here. Do you think one of these would fit in your belly?"

Siman looked at the mahogany trees around him.

"But you said an apple tree would grow in my belly," he said. "So, it would be smaller, then?"

"Until it grew! Then it would burst your belly, wouldn't it?"

"O," he said.

He spent a few minutes looking at his apple core and then the mahogany trees, and back again.

Then he asked "Igran, where should apple trees grow?"

"In the ground, of course."

"Like these trees?" he asked.

He stood up and went to the nearest tree and looked down to where its trunk emerged between slabs of rough concrete and a small circle of clay. He leant over and poked the clay with his finger, and then studied the apple core. Igran came to join him.

"You know, every now and then you don't seem so stupid," she said.

"We could have apples all the time," he said.

"This could be the new plan we need," she said.

"Should I just put it on the ground?"

"Not here," she said. "This tree's taken up all the space."

So, they took Mummy's core from her for good measure, and they went off to find a suitable space for their new orchard.

It was hard to find any patch of bare ground, anywhere. They finally found some dirt beside a newly constructed office building set back from Ortalt Ave; much of the building debris remained, chunks of concrete and brick that hadn't undergone the old-man's-futility process yet, but there was exposed ground here and there, and even some sprigs of green trying to grow. Igran stood over one such space and pronounced it the very spot for their tree.

"What do we do?" Siman asked.

"Well, clear off the space, so there's only nice dirt there."

He knelt down and brushed at it a bit, but then admitted he couldn't tell which was the nice dirt and which wasn't.

"Just leave the dirt you'd like to lie down on, yourself," she advised.

"I wouldn't like to lie down on any of it."

"Here," she said, kneeling beside him. She swept some of the dirt aside, and then patted what remained. "There. All nice. Give me the apples."

Siman handed the three cores to her, and she laid them neatly, side by side, and settled back onto her little haunches.

"What now?" he asked.

"Now we wait," she said.

Siman sat himself down and watched the cores carefully.

"Nothing's happening," he said eventually.

"Not yet," Igran said. "It will take time."

"Maybe they should be turned the other way."

"Siman, what do you know about trees?" she demanded.

"Nothing," said the boy who knew only that he knew nothing about anything.

"Exactly," affirmed the girl who might not even know that.

Quite some time later, Siman observed that the cores were turning brown a bit, a colour rather similar to tree trunks, so that was a promising sign to him. The cores, he thought, were somewhat the same shape as trees, too, so he pictured they would simply darken and enlarge, the widened top sprouting green, before his eyes. But even as he was finding reason to hope, Igran sighed, leaned forward, and turned the cores over.

"There should be something by now," she said.

They settled into their vigil, until their minds wandered, and their vision lost focus, and the motors and horns and exhausts of Ortalt overpowered their senses into a stupor. After what seemed a very long time, Siman's observation was activated again by what appeared to be a rust-brown rippling of the surface of the cores.

"Igran, they're starting!"

"At last!" said Igran, and they both bent over them in inspection.

"Wait," Siman said. "What is that?"

"Ants!" cried Igran. "Ants!"

And, indeed, it became clear that the cores were completely covered in tiny, milling red ants.

"They're growing ants?" Siman asked. "What kind of apples ---?"

"No, no! Ants are trying to steal them from us. We have to stop them."

Siman picked up one core and shook it vigorously. No ants fell off, but several climbed onto his thumb and started along his bare arm, giving little bites as they went. He dropped the core and rubbed his arm hard, curling the little ant agonists, not at all mindful that he might be fulfilling Igran's dictum of killing that which hurt them.

Igran spit on a core, and that seemed to discourage the raiders, so both children spit and spit; their supply of saliva was soon spent, though. The exercise was sufficient to make them reluctant to touch the cores again.

"Pour dirt on them!" said Igran in inspiration. "That will keep the ants off them!"

Siman scooped up handfuls of earth and dropped them on the cores, patting them down. That seemed too much attention for the ants, and they filed way.

"Will the tree grow, though?" Siman asked.

"We'll have to wait and see."

And wait they did, but didn't see, until the shadows lengthened, and they followed them too far into silent thought for such a time. At one point, Igran leant forward to shout "Grow, you stupid tree, grow!", and Siman, speaking from familial experience, said that calling it stupid wouldn't help.

Finally, as dusk fell, Igran stood up.

"This is hopeless," she said, spitefully kicking more dirt onto that covering the cores. "You stupid apples are useless!"

And, as colours drained, they made their way back to Mummy's camp.

It's for us to understand that what may appear to be a success may later prove to be a failure, and what may appear to be a failure may prove out a success. Igran and Siman were never to know of the tree that grew where they inadvertently planted. And as ye sow, so someone else may reap, someone such as the peon of the office building who was perplexed to find, many weeks later, the sapling struggling there, and who nurtured it until, some dutiful years after that, he had occasional apples to supplement the meagre diet of his poor son and daughter. He thanked Pakron, and then he thanked Pazich for a spell, then went back to thanking Pakron, but he never thanked Igran or Siman; on the contrary, one day he would come to curse

Igran's name. However, he would hardly be singular in doing that.

By the time they returned to Mummy, she was already asleep under the cloth, having cleaned their area of chicken parts and feathers and settled down. Siman lay beside her, and had an impulse to hug her, but something of the presentation of her back seemed unwelcoming.

Igran lay beside him and snuggled up, shivering.

Many snatches of the day played their little tunes in Siman's head, but one from the man who bought shingaras presented itself to the forefront.

"Igran, was I not alive always?"

"Let me think," said Igran, and she pondered a while. "I've always been alive, but I don't know about you. You're very little, but I remember when you were even punier, and before that... well, I don't know where you were, but you weren't with us, maybe. There are some babies who are born, you know, out of their mothers' bellies."

"I know that," said Siman with a little shudder.

Overt talk of reproduction was considered sinful by the Fannu faithful, and the children's knowledge was limited to unexplained observations and independent deductions and the wild rumours from other children.

"It's horrible, but true," Igran said. "Maybe you were one of those."

"I hope not," he said.

"Yes, of course you do. I sure won't ever let a baby do that to me. But I think you might be one of them."

"I think maybe those are just rich babies," he said.

"No, no, some poor babies, too. Something made Mummy so weird; that's probably what. Where you were before that, I just don't know."

"Not alive?"

"Maybe not."

He drifted off trying to remember not being alive.

The children were awakened the next early morning by a sound they hated to hear, that of Mummy's shrill voice of denunciation as she engaged interminable condemnation of whomever was her tormenter of the instant.

As they sat up and cleared their own vestigial torments of the night from their eyes, wondering whom it might be who'd aroused Mummy's ire, they came to see that the circumstance of it was something different, for Mummy, standing on the footpath, had no visible adversary before her. She flounced and flaunted in her manner of combat, wagging her head and splaying her hair and thrusting out breast and hips in ruthless emphasis of her lethal weapon femininity, and she gestured with spread fingers and shook her shoulders. Her gestures were clearly aimed at the centre of the road, and there was, as clearly, no one there.

Siman recognized the content of her diatribe, absorbed unwittingly the first time he'd heard it. It was, approximately word for word, her side of her quarrel with Rachan, re-enacted accurately complete with fuming interruptions for Rachan's rejoinders.

Guards from the surrounding buildings gathered into a semi-circle about the raving woman, at first with a simple need for the rant's entertainment, but soon they were, most of them, overtaken by a woeful pity, and what had promised to be a diversion from their normally uneventful days became a spectacle most would have preferred to avoid, especially when they saw the wretched children sitting by the strutting lunatic.

For little Siman, that was his limit and beyond, more cumulative pain and misery than he could endure. He looked to his sister and her expression of shame and woe, and her misery compounded his. He'd thought, the night before, of not having lived; he hadn't succeeded in remembering not being alive, but he felt sure it was less unhappy and frightening than his current state of being alive. So he cast his gaze away, up to the top of Royal Towers, and that was solely to speculate as to his necessary release by climbing its stairs --- though he'd never climbed stairs and couldn't guess he'd be any good at it --- while the guard was absent and occupied by Mummy's fascinating spectacle, and throwing himself from its heights, to seek the relief of his rich imagination at least, if in no other way.

When he looked to the very top, seeking the promise of his delivery, to the ledge that ran along the top of Royal Towers' wall, he saw not himself, but rather a little glint that caught his eye. And as he watched it, it grew from that tiny spark into a sort of radiance that shot out beams at his eyes as though they were aimed. He cried out in initial alarm, and looked to Igran and tugged at her arm, but she was resolute in her examination of the dirt at her bare feet. He was as unable to keep his gaze from the phenomenon at the top of the building, and he looked back to it, and found himself no longer alarmed, but both excited and soothed at the same time, for there seemed to emanate from it not only that which might be seen, but that which might be felt and that which might be, somehow, inarticulately but profoundly understood, as though by invitation rather than invasion, as though it fully came to him only as he fully came to it.

This surely was, he thought, something intended for Mummy's relief, somehow the answer to her arguments that would satisfy her and carry her to solace and transport her from her embattled anguish; but he was wrong in that surmise, too selfless and modest in his assessment of his world and his place in it.

He stood and took Mummy's hand and tried to capture her infuriated eye, tried to direct, by way of his pointing finger, her angry kite eye up to the inexplicable but utterly understood radiance at the top of the building, so she could be reassured as he was reassured, comforted as he was comforted, thrilled as he was thrilled.

But it wasn't for her, and she wouldn't look. So he held her arm, that same thing that had cost his father his life, so that he might redeem hers, that the wonder of what he saw might be transmitted through him to her, and he stood quaking, elated in the full emanation of the glowing mystery that crowned Royal Towers.

He did marvel.

And, as if his hand were divinely directed, he reached into the pocket of his shabby little shorts, and there, in the lower front corner of his pocket, lodged in a hole not quite large enough to allow its passage through, was a glassy little globe, and he extracted it: it was a last marble, blue with swirling white like a perfect world.

He held the marble up to the mystery, and it lent it luminescence and glowing depths that must be explored.

Now seven-year-old Siman says, "I know what I saw." But that isn't entirely true; knowing that one saw something isn't the same as knowing what one saw. With one hand in his pocket, he holds his blue marble, ready to pull it out and gaze through it to his thrill and to the very depths of his essential need to know, and with his other hand he clasps his brow, and, looking to the top of Royal Tower, he marvels.

"We're never going to get anything to eat," Igran says sharply from her squat.

"We have to feed our hearts, too," says Siman, "don't we?"

"You feed your heart, I'll feed my belly, and we'll see who's still around to tell about it."

She stands up and scuffs her bare feet in the grit just to do it, maybe warming up her feet for good traction when needed.

Siman glances over to her, then looks back up, but, where he seeks wonder, he finds horror, for, from the top of the tower roof suddenly fly two children, two children spinning and flapping in desperate discovery that they can't live even as the birds do.

Siman issues a shout of alarm, has time to see that the smaller of the two children is plummeting directly toward him, the larger toward Igran, and he reaches up his arms to catch the child, reaches up his arms like they're the limbs of a miracle tree, even as he realizes that their fates are now one, that their meeting point is their focal mutual destruction, still he stands in resolute reception.

This may be the pivotal point where parallel lines can't meet, but do.

This may be the pivotal point where forward-reaching time, ever upward like a miracle tree, suddenly spins around and streaks back to find where it once was. What force can bring time about?

This is the pivotal point where we spin our gaze away, can't bring ourselves to look, because that's our nature: we coil and recoil, we reel from what's real for two or maybe four children as they must stare into the glare of their fate, we wish to look away, not in apathy, but in sympathy.

Mummy is long gone in pursuit of that which only she can construe. Displaced even from the slum of their birth, the children are as the stray dogs. They can listen with envy or pleasure to the birds that share the brief allowance of their early morning, but, for all that they flap, they can't live even as the birds do.

So, this is the thing about pivotal points: the world is, indeed, round, and it spins like a top on its pivotal point, and that spinning, that movement, that sequential light and dark, those seasons that come and go, make winds, and the winds blow, and most lives are spent hiding behind false feeble fortress walls, defending against the critical mistrals and mistrials of those winds, why, many even burrow underground and seek to sacrifice all the light and marvels and marbles to shield against those winds; but some lives the winds wind like tops they haven't really won, and send them spinning, who knows where, on capricious dancing pivotal points, so that those of such lives can only look and wish and hope at where they long to go, glance and bounce off all the grit and pit and stones and bit of broken brick that impede and send them off on tangents: is this divinely directed?

In an instant, as he looks up, Siman registers a ghastly recognition without understanding. He knows the form of the boy plummeting to him, knows it only too terribly well, but not the meaning.

For our part, we may know we've seen something of Siman and Igran, but can we know what we've seen? To know anything for sure, if that's at all possible, if that's at all desirable, we must risk a little, must marshal our sympathy, must follow farther, must follow spontaneously the erratic path of Siman and Igran and where the wind spun them.